THE CATALPA
ADVENTURE
ESCAPE TO FREEDOM

VINCENT McDONNELL

The Collins Press

For my sister Kathy, Tommy and family and my sister Pat, Peter and family. Thanks for showing us Manhattan and the lights of Broadway.

FIRST PUBLISHED IN 2010 BY
The Collins Press
West Link Park
Doughcloyne
Wilton
Cork

A Cataloguing in Publication data record for this book is available from the British Library

ISBN: 978-1848890381

Typesetting by The Collins Press
Typeset in Bembo 12 pt and Candara 16 pt
Printed in Ireland by ColourBooks Ltd

Contents

By the same author

Michael Collins: Most Wanted Man
Titanic Tragedy
The Story of the GAA

Vincent McDonnell is from County Mayo and now lives near Newmarket, County Cork. In 1989 he won the GPA First Fiction Award, after being recommended by Graham Greene. He has published three other non-fiction titles and five novels for children. The winner of numerous prizes, he has been writer in residence at many venues and has given workshops and readings all over Ireland.

1

Bound in Chains

The morning of 12 October 1867 was wet and bitterly cold. In Portland Prison in England, sixty-three Irish Fenian prisoners slept huddled beneath thin blankets. Suddenly a din outside their cells – the thump of warders' boots and their shouts and curses – roused the prisoners from their uneasy sleep.

The cell doors were unbolted and flung open. 'Out! Out!' the warders screamed. The prisoners threw off their threadbare blankets, scrambled from their beds and hurried out on to the landings. As they did so, they were thumped and kicked. Groans and cries of pain carried on the stinking air.

Among the sixty-three prisoners were six men who had been convicted of treason against the British queen. They were Robert Cranston from Stewartstown, County Tyrone, Thomas Darragh from Broomhall, Rathnew, County Wicklow, Michael Harrington from Cork city, Thomas Hassett of Doneraile in County Cork, Martin Hogan from Limerick city and James Wilson from Newry in County Down. These six men were destined to be part of one of the greatest seafaring adventures of all time – The Catalpa Rescue.

Because they were regarded as traitors, they were treated more harshly than the common prisoners, though many of these were notorious murderers, robbers and thieves. The six were dragged from their beds by shouting warders, beaten and kicked and forced out on to the landings.

Here, they were lined up according to their prison numbers. Now, two of the six Fenian prisoners found themselves together. These were Thomas Hassett, Prisoner No. 9757, and Michael Harrington, Prisoner No. 9758. 'What's happening?' they whispered to each other, but neither man knew.

Bewildered, the two men stood shivering in the bitter cold. Warders moved along the line handing the prisoners their breakfasts. This consisted of cold potato-and-oat porridge, a hunk of bread and a mug of bitter cocoa. For men in the prime of life, the food hardly sated their ravenous appetites.

Both men, like their four fellow Fenians, had spent months in prisons in Ireland and England. They had suffered hunger and beatings and harsh working conditions. Already they were showing signs of this ill-treatment.

Now soldiers dragging iron chains moved along the lines of prisoners. Each prisoner was attached to the chains by wrists and ankles according to his number, twenty prisoners to each chain. Many were suffering from cuts and sores on their ankles and wrists caused by being previously shackled. Their groans and cries of pain echoed around the bleak prison walls.

To the clanking of chains, the prisoners were driven out into the prison yard. Within minutes they were soaked through by the driving rain and stood hunched against the bitter wind blowing off Portland Harbour. All around them the prison buildings and its high encircling stone wall loomed against the dark skyline.

Prisoners whispered among themselves, all wondering what was happening. 'Silence!' the soldiers and warders screamed as they strode along the lines, punching and kicking those who did not obey.

Then word passed among the prisoners. They were being transported to Fremantle, in Western Australia. A ship was lying at anchor in Portland Harbour to take them on the 24,000-kilometre journey across two of the most dangerous oceans in the world.

The six Fenian prisoners greeted the news with horror. Sentenced to penal servitude for life, they knew that once they reached Australia they would never again be free men. They would never return to their beloved country, Ireland, nor would they ever be reunited with their families.

Suddenly an order rang out: 'Convicts: Forward March!' Drums began to beat. The prisoners – Fenians and common prisoners alike – shuffled toward the opening gates of the prison, their chains jangling. They trudged out the gate and down the cobbled road toward the harbour. Soldiers with fixed bayonets marched alongside both groups. The six Fenians marched to the drumbeat. As former soldiers in the British army, they still retained their professional pride.

A crowd had gathered to watch the prisoners being herded to the waiting ship. Among the crowd were friends and relatives of the prisoners. Now they shouted goodbyes to their loved ones. A young girl rushed forward and tried to embrace her brother, but a soldier caught her and flung her back.

Soldiers struck out at any prisoner who spoke or did not keep up. Desperate cries of pain and loss mingled with the beat of the drums and the clanking of the chains. On they marched, or stumbled, to the quayside. Here, a paddle steamer waited to transport the prisoners to the ship.

Prisoners being herded to the waiting ship.
GARETH HAYES, AGED 15

Bound in Chains

The prisoners were forced to board the paddle steamer. Shouts and oaths and curses rent the air. Eventually, all the prisoners were crammed on board. With black smoke puffing into the dark sky, the paddle steamer pulled away from the quay.

In the distance, through the rain, Hassett and Harrington and the four other Fenians saw the dark bulk of the ship that would take them to Australia. As they approached, they could read the name on her side. She was the *Hougoumont*, a large merchantman, which had been converted to a convict ship. Painted on her dark hull was a white arrow, which indicated her status.

Men dressed in red uniforms and cradling rifles lined her decks. These were former British soldiers who had agreed to go to Australia with their families. They would be paid a pension for doing so and were known as pensioners. During the long voyage they would guard the prisoners and help to keep order on board.

The paddle steamer pulled alongside the *Hougoumont* and was made fast. Prodded by bayonets, the prisoners scrambled on board. Here, they were unchained and, surrounded by hostile soldiers, stood in the wind and driving rain. Many of them begged for water, but were refused. Anyone who protested was beaten with rifle butts.

Two hatches in the ship's main deck stood open. Iron cages with heavy doors had been erected at the entrance to each hatch. Armed soldiers flanked the doors. One by one, the prisoners' numbers were called. Each prisoner stepped forward and clambered down a ladder into the ship's dark hold.

Here the murk was emphasised by a few sputtering oil lamps. Prisoner after prisoner descended into the darkness, where already the stench of wet clothing and sweat and fear added to the already fetid air. Eventually, when all the prisoners were below, the hatches were closed.

Down in the gloomy hold the cries and screams of fear, anger and pain of the prisoners resounded. Fights broke out as men sought the best places in which to lie down. The Fenian prisoners remained together. Though some of them had been soldiers, they were still wary of the other convicts, many of whom were guilty of terrible crimes.

As the tumult continued, a clanking, screeching sound filled the air as the anchors were raised. Then the ship's timbers groaned as if the vessel was alive. She began to roll as the sails were unfurled and she began to tack away from Portland Harbour. Soon the degree of roll increased as she cleared the harbour and entered the English Channel.

The six Fenian prisoners believed just then that they would never return, but were destined to die in prison in Australia. It was also the belief of many of the fifty-seven other Fenians, some of whom would die in prison and be buried in Australia. Others would eventually be released. Some of those remained in Australia while some returned to Ireland or went to America.

One of the fifty-seven Fenians, John Boyle O'Reilly, was destined to escape from prison in Australia within two years and make his way to America. There, with other Fenians, he helped plan The Catalpa Rescue.

Yet that October morning, as the *Hougoumont* sailed into the English Channel, neither Harrington nor Hassett, nor the other four Fenians, had any dreams of escape. They did not then know that within nine years they would be part of The Catalpa Rescue, one of the most daring sea adventures of all.

In April 1876, they made a bold escape from Fremantle

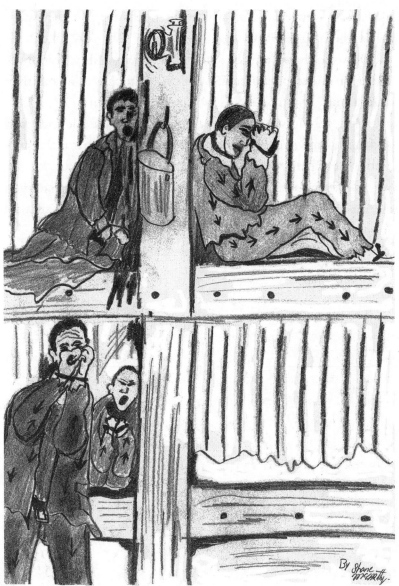

In the Hougoumont*'s dark hold.*
SHANE MCCARTHY, AGED 14

Prison in Western Australia. They evaded capture, survived a storm and perilous danger from a British ship intent on recapturing them, before boarding a whaling ship bound for America. The ship was the *Catalpa*, one of the most famous ships of all time.

This is the story of that adventure, one of the most exciting and daring and dangerous rescues ever undertaken. It is the story of the brave men who planned the rescue and those, braver still, who carried it out. It is a story of great courage and self-sacrifice. Above all, it is the story of those six Fenian prisoners who survived in the harshest prison in Australia, and who one day sailed to freedom and a new life in America.

2

Prisoners in Despair

With the *Hougoumont* pitching and rolling in the choppy seas, the prisoners quickly experienced life on a convict ship. Many had never been to sea before and were seasick. Buckets, provided as toilet facilities, soon overflowed. Within hours, the hold stank worse than ever. The air was thick with the sounds of retching and cries of distress and despair.

Conditions were even worse for the Fenians, especially the former soldiers. The crew and the pensioner guards singled out the Fenians for harsh treatment. Because they had been convicted of treason, they were regarded as traitors.

Yet they thought of themselves, not as traitors, but as patriots. They felt that they owed no allegiance to an English queen, only to their own country, Ireland. It was because of their love of their country and their wish to see it free of English rule that they were now prisoners.

For 700 years, Ireland had been ruled by England. During the 700 years there had been many rebellions in Ireland to try and win freedom for the people. Following these rebellions, England had treated the Irish population with great brutality. Many rebels were hanged or forced into exile. Their lands were confiscated and given to Englishmen as a reward for helping to put down the rebellions.

Most of those Irish people who lost their lands now lived on the verge of starvation. Many became labourers on the settlers' estates. Others obtained work as servants. All of these were desperately poor and barely had enough to eat.

Others who lost their lands now rented land from the new English settlers, or landlords, at a very high rent. As the population grew, the land was divided up into smaller farms. Much of the land was used to grow grain, which was then sold to pay the rent. What little land remained was used to grow potatoes to feed the family.

By 1800, the potato had become the main food source for the majority of Irish peasants. The potato, though, was prone to a disease known as potato blight. This could destroy a whole crop overnight, leaving a family without food. They could not eat the grain because that had to be sold to pay the rent. If the rent wasn't paid, the family would be evicted and their home destroyed.

From time to time, the potato crop partly failed, bringing famine to many areas. But then in the years 1845 to 1847 blight became widespread. As the potato crop failed each year, a terrible famine spread throughout the country. More than a million people died of hunger or disease, or emigrated to Britain or America.

Those who went to America did not forget Ireland or the plight of her people. One of these was a Limerick man, John O'Mahony. With other like-minded Irishmen he founded a secret society in America in 1858. He named it the Fenian Brotherhood after the ancient Irish heroes of legend, The Fianna. Its aim was to organise another rebellion in Ireland.

Prisoners in Despair

While O'Mahony was organising his society in New York, a Kilkenny man named James Stephens was setting up a similar secret organisation in Ireland. This was the Irish Republican Brotherhood (IRB). Both men made contact with each other and Stephens planned for a rebellion in Ireland in 1865.

He claimed that up to 200,000 men would be available to fight. Many of those were in Ireland. Others would come from America. These were the experienced Irish soldiers who had just fought in the American Civil War. This rebellion would have one other advantage over previous rebellions. Stephens and his colleagues had also recruited thousands of Irishmen who were soldiers in the British army. All these trained soldiers would be a match for the soldiers the English government would use to try and suppress the rebellion.

But before a date was set for the rebellion, Stephens was arrested in November 1865 and imprisoned in Richmond Prison in Dublin. But his fellow Fenians helped him escape and afterwards he fled to France. Among those who had organised the escape were John Devoy and John J. Breslin. Eleven years later they would play a vital part in The Catalpa Rescue.

Acting on information from informers, the authorities now arrested and tried hundreds of Fenians. Those found guilty of membership of the IRB received prison sentences. Fenians who were members of the British army were tried for treason. Those found guilty were sentenced to be hanged.

However, the authorities did not carry out the death sentences. Instead, they decided to transport those men, as well as other convicted Fenians, to Australia. This was how in October 1867, sixty-three Fenians found themselves on the *Hougoumont*, bound for Fremantle, Australia.

The *Catalpa* Adventure

Fremantle Prison had been chosen because it was the most secure prison in Australia. Even if a man escaped from the prison, he had no hope of getting any further. On one side, the prison was bounded by a vast wilderness of bush and desert. No man could survive for long in that harsh, waterless land where temperatures could reach nearly a scorching 50 degrees.

On the other side of the prison lay the vast Indian Ocean. There was no need for men to guard this expanse of water. Looking out from shore one could see dark triangular fins cutting through the water. These fins belonged to killer sharks, which could bite a man in two with one snap of their razor-sharp teeth.

Satisfied that none of the Fenians would ever escape from Fremantle Prison, the British authorities were feeling more than satisfied. Yet, in October 1867, as the *Hougoumont* sailed on with its human cargo, the authorities could not imagine that in less than ten years one of the most daring sea rescues ever would take place. Or that six of the men locked away like animals in the hold of the convict ship would become some of the most famous Irish prison escapees of all time.

3
Storm at Sea

As days and weeks passed, life on board the *Hougoumont* settled into a routine. The Fenian soldiers, who had been put with the common criminals, were allowed to join the civilian Fenians. Here, they felt more secure amongst their own. The civilians were allowed books and these they shared with the soldiers.

Then a rumour began to circulate among the prisoners. It claimed that a ship, manned by American Fenians, would intercept the *Hougoumont* and rescue the prisoners. This rumour was fuelled by the presence of the British gunship, HMS *Earnest*. The prisoners assumed that it was there to prevent any such attempt. But as time passed, no vessel came to the rescue. Instead, danger came from another quarter.

The Atlantic is a turbulent ocean. Storms regularly rage there. Now a storm raged as the *Hougoumont* sailed through the Bay of Biscay. For days, mountainous seas battered the ship. Giant waves washed over the decks and flooded the hold. The wind howled and shrieked in the rigging and ripped sails to shreds. The ship pitched and rolled continuously, making life on board almost unbearable.

Down in the hold the creaks and groans of the ship's timbers matched the groans and cries of the convicts. Again, many were

Caught in a storm in the Bay of Biscay.
JOANNE BROPHY, AGED 15

violently seasick. Others cowered in fear, certain that they were going to die. If the ship capsized, or was swamped with water, it would sink and they would be drowned, trapped in the darkness like rats.

No cooking could be done and the prisoners and crew and guards had to eat what could be provided. Neither could the prisoners go up on deck to take their half hour of exercise. During their exercise, the Fenian soldiers had marched around the deck. This had drawn admiration from the guards, who began to treat the soldiers less harshly.

After three days, the storm abated. Now the prisoners were forced to clean up the stinking, filthy hold. Afterwards they were allowed on deck once more and able to breathe clean fresh air.

While on deck, the prisoners could not but be aware of the means of punishment on board. Two iron rings were attached to the mast while a third ring was attached to the deck. Anyone who disobeyed the rules would have his hands and feet tied to the rings and then flogged. At the ship's bow there was a punishment cell with thick iron bars. Hanging from the mast above the iron rings was a rope, known as the 'hempen halter'. This was for the ultimate punishment of hanging.

After the storm had died down, HMS *Earnest* turned about and headed for home, leaving the *Hougoumont* alone on the vast ocean. Many of the Fenians were bitterly disappointed that their American allies had not come to their rescue. Now they considered taking over the *Hougoumont* and sailing it to America.

But this plan raised many problems. Even if they took control of the ship, what were they to do with the crew and the soldiers on board? While they were willing to fight to take over the ship, they could never consider killing in cold blood. There was also the problem of what to do with the other convicts. While the American authorities might allow the Fenian prisoners into the country, they would not wish to admit those notorious criminals.

There was much heated argument about such a plan. All were aware of the dangers involved. If they failed, they would be tried and hanged. For the soldiers, who faced life in prison, this prospect did not seem too desperate. But for the civilian Fenians, who would be freed when they had served their sentences, hanging was not an attractive prospect. Even if they successfully seized the ship, they would be branded as common criminals and would never be able to return to their homes.

After much bitter debate, a vote was taken. The civilian Fenians voted against the plan. The soldiers were deeply disappointed, but without the support of the civilians they could not hope to take over the ship.

Resigned to their fate, they were forced to make the most of life on board. For the former soldiers, boredom was almost as difficult to endure as captivity. To relieve the monotony they organised concert parties below decks. At these they sang Irish songs and recited poems. Some of the prisoners, like John Boyle O'Reilly and Denis Cashman, wrote poems, which they recited. These poems were about Ireland's fight for freedom and the hope that soon she would be free.

William Cozens, the captain of the *Hougoumont*, knew that boredom on a ship could lead to violence and was determined to prevent this. As the parties helped to relieve tedium, he was willing to allow them.

The *Hougoumont* eventually reached Funchal on the island of Madeira, where she docked. After taking on water and food and other vital supplies, she sailed once more. Her next port of call was Fremantle, still over 20,000 kilometres away across the vast expanse of the Atlantic and Indian Oceans.

4
Land Ahoy!

As the *Hougoumont* sailed further south the heat became more oppressive. Down in the hold it was stifling hot and the hatches were opened to allow in fresh air. The only relief was when the prisoners were allowed on deck for exercise. Here, they had a brief glimpse of the burning sun in a clear blue sky before they were again forced down into the hold at bayonet point.

The heat brought other problems. The meat went bad and the water turned rancid. The good meat and clean water were given to the ship's crew and guards while the prisoners had to make do with the rotting meat and tainted water.

Even then the rations were hardly enough to keep a man alive. The prisoners suffered greatly from hunger and thirst. They complained to William Smith, the doctor on board. But he was an uncaring man and their complaints went unanswered.

The doctor treated those who were ill with similar indifference. But he reserved his greatest indifference for the Fenian prisoners. Their complaints and illnesses were utterly ignored.

The Fenian soldiers protested about the food and refused to obey the officers in charge. This would normally have led to their being punished, either by flogging or serving time in the prison cell. But the captain took note of their protest and ordered that better food and water be supplied to the convicts.

To help cope with the boredom, the Fenians started a newspaper called *Wild Goose*. It contained their handwritten poems and songs and other writings. Readings from this newspaper now became part of the concerts on board.

One morning, a convict named Thomas Corcoran was found dead. His death was a stark reminder to the prisoners of what fate might also befall them. The dead man's body was put in a sack and convicts hauled it up on deck. Father Delany, the priest on board, held a funeral service before Thomas Corcoran's body was thrown overboard to a watery grave.

For a while gloom descended on the prisoners. But it was close to Christmas and they began to look forward to the day. On Christmas Day 1867, the prisoners held a concert party, where the *Wild Goose* was read. It was the final edition, as they would soon arrive in Australia.

With a mood of expectation and dread on board, the *Hougoumont* sailed on. Then, on the morning of 10 January 1868, land was sighted. After a voyage of around 24,000 kilometres, the ship and her human cargo had reached Australia.

When the prisoners came up on deck they had their first glimpse of the country. Shimmering in the heat haze, it seemed harsh and inhospitable. They could see in the distance the white lighthouse on Rottnest Island and the white glare off the buildings of Fremantle.

The prisoners presented a sorry sight in the bright sunshine. Months in the dark hold of the *Hougoumont* had reduced them to skeletal wrecks. Washing facilities had been of a primitive nature and they all stank of stale sweat. Their clothing was tattered and dirty and infested with fleas and lice. Many were suffering from sores and sickness. Others had injuries received in fights, or from being tossed about in the storms.

The *Hougoumont* now made its way into the Swan River Estuary. Out beyond the estuary, the fins of killer sharks could be seen knifing through the water. Slowly the barren countryside appeared more clearly out of the haze. As the ship drew nearer to the shore, the prisoners had to shade their eyes from the sun's glare off the white buildings of Fremantle. These buildings, built of sandstone and limestone, would soon become a permanent, familiar and depressing sight.

First glimpse of Fremantle Prison.
DARREN MCCORMACK, AGED 14

But an even more depressing and forbidding sight was the their first glimpse of Fremantle Prison. It stood on a rise above the town, starkly white in the glare of the sun. The fortress-like building was three storeys high and shaped like a giant letter E. High walls surrounded it and twin towers guarded the only entrance gate.

The prison could house 1,000 convicts. The regime within was harsh and brutal. Discipline was strictly enforced by flogging, solitary confinement and a bread and water diet. Not only had the prisoners to contend with these conditions, but they were also expected to work clearing brush and building roads, bridges and jetties. In this sort of regime, with poor food and hard work in extreme heat, the life expectancy of a prisoner was not good.

As the *Hougoumont* dropped anchor, a steamer drew near. On board were pensioner guards and heavily armed water police. The steamer also carried two important men, who now boarded the *Hougoumont*. One of these was Doctor John Stephen Hampton, Governor of Western Australia. The other was Henry Wakeford who would be in charge of the prisoners in Fremantle Prison.

The prisoners were cursorily examined by a doctor and deemed to be fit and well. Now the order was given that they be taken from the ship and transferred to the prison. Under the watchful eyes of the pensioners and the water police, the prisoners' numbers were called out. One by one they made their way down improvised gangplanks onto barges, which would take them ashore.

On the jetty, the prisoners were lined up in single file and marched off to the prison. As they marched through Fremantle, everywhere they looked there was the same dazzling white of buildings and streets and pavements. Many of the locals, who were Irish and had Fenian sympathies, watched the prisoners as they marched by.

The prisoners marched up the hill to the prison. Here, guards atop the gate towers watched for signs of trouble. The long line of prisoners entered the prison courtyard where again everything was a blinding white.

The prisoners underwent another quick medical examination. Then while they stood in the searing heat, Henry Wakeford addressed them. He read the prison rules and detailed the punishments, which would be meted out to any prisoner who broke them. These were floggings, solitary confinement, time added to the sentence and ultimately death by hanging.

Wakeford warned them of the futility of trying to escape. On the landward side a prisoner would die of thirst or sunstroke or from the bite of a poisonous snake before ever reaching freedom. On the seaward side the shark-infested waters were a guarantee of certain death for anyone who tried to swim out to a ship. Even if one could steal a boat, what lay beyond was the vast Indian Ocean. Again, no one could survive out there.

Most of the ships that plied these waters were British. No captain would take on board an escaped convict. 'You are prisoners here,' Wakeford said, 'and prisoners you will remain until you have served your sentence, or until you die.'

For the six Fenian prisoners, his harsh words seemed to sound their death knell. Sentenced to life imprisonment for treason, they would die here in this dazzling white fortress unless they escaped. But right now, that prospect seemed hopeless and death seemed to offer the only way out.

5
In Fremantle Prison

Now, as the prisoners entered the prison, their spirits sank further. For the six Fenian soldiers, this would be the only home they would know until they died. So though it was cool within the stone building, this brought the men little relief.

Once inside, they were marched to the prison washrooms. Here, they removed their filthy, stinking clothes and washed in wooden troughs, which were used as baths. After washing off months of sweat and dirt, the prisoners were issued with prison clothing, known as Drogheda linen. They received vests, shirts, socks, trousers and boots, along with a jacket and a hat. Both the jacket and trousers bore a red stripe, black bands and coloured arrows, denoting that the wearer was a convict.

After this, the prisoners made their way to the mess hall to eat. The food consisted of meat, boiled potatoes, bread and a mug of unsweetened warm chocolate. Once they had eaten, the Fenian soldiers, including the six who would eventually escape on the *Catalpa*, were separated from the civilians. Each soldier was put in a single cell and the corrugated iron door slammed shut and locked.

The cell was tiny, barely a metre wide, three metres long and two metres high. The walls were whitewashed and the floors and ceilings were of wood. There were no beds. Instead, each prisoner had a hammock and a thin blanket. A wooden bucket held water for washing and a urinal was also supplied. A hinged shelf hung on the wall. It could be raised, propped on one leg, and used as a table. The single window was set so high in the wall that the prisoners could not see out.

For the soldiers, used to living in barracks, the cells were confining. Barely two strides took a man from one end to the other. If he threw out his broad shoulders they would touch the walls on either side. Here the men felt as if they had already been entombed.

Resigned to their fate for now, and with feelings of anger and despair, the soldiers climbed into their hammocks that first night. Most of them were unable to sleep at first. Around them, those who did sleep cried out in their nightmares.

Sleep eventually claimed them. But it seemed as if they had hardly fallen asleep before the clanging of the prison bell woke them. It was 4.30 a.m. and still dark. To the shouts of the warders and the thump of their boots, the men tumbled out of their hammocks and washed in cold water.

Keys rattled in iron locks and the cell doors swung open. Each man, carrying his urinal, marched out to the prison yard and emptied the container. Then he returned to his cell until summoned for breakfast at 5.30 a.m. This consisted of bread, gruel and warm cocoa, and did satisfy the men's appetites at all.

After breakfast, they were ordered to the chapel. Here, Father Lynch, the prison chaplain, prayed with the prisoners. Once the prayers were said, the prisoners were returned to their solitary cells where they were locked up almost permanently for the next few days.

So it was with some relief that they were eventually sent to work gangs out in the bush. The authorities, fearing that they might plot to escape, assigned them to separate gangs.

In the gangs they found themselves chained to common criminals – murderers and robbers and thieves. Their work was to clear brush and quarry stone to build roads and bridges and jetties. From dawn until dusk they toiled in the intense heat. In temperatures that could reach nearly 50 degrees, any exposed skin was first burned red raw. Later it took on the colour and texture of leather.

Swinging a sledgehammer to break stones, or working a saw cutting down trees day after day, soon sapped the men's strength. The fierce glare of the sun also seared their eyes. There was no twilight and the sun set quickly. This sudden onset of darkness after the harsh glare caused an eye problem known as moon blindness. Most men suffered from this to some degree. Other types of injuries were common and there was little or no medical treatment.

The nights they spent out in the bush brought no relief. Some prisoners had hammocks but did not have blankets. Others slept in makeshift huts made of brush, or in tents. Other prisoners slept chained together out in the open. Mosquito bites added to their discomfort, as did the scourge of fleas. Poisonous snakes were plentiful and a bite from one could cause a prisoner to suffer an agonising death.

The long days became weeks and the weeks became months. Day after long day the prisoners laboured on, their strength slowly waning. The food was still poor and men grew thin and gaunt; many were little more than skeletons covered in skin.

As the months passed, the six Fenians came to realise that

their only hope of survival lay in escape. If they remained as prisoners they would die. Convicted of treason and sentenced to penal servitude for life, they knew that there would be no remission of their sentences. While the civilian Fenians had some hope of one day being free, the soldiers knew that they were doomed to die in chains.

But there seemed little prospect of escape. Even if a man got away from his work gang and escaped into the bush he would be tracked down and dragged back in chains. The authorities used Aboriginal trackers, native men who could track a prisoner over solid rock. Even if a prisoner escaped the trackers, he would quickly die of thirst out in the wilderness.

The ocean offered no better prospect. A man could drown if the sharks didn't take him. Even if he made it to a passing ship, no captain would take on board an escaped convict. Any escaped prisoner would have a price put on his head and there were many released convicts who would have no scruples in betraying a man in order to get the bounty.

With little prospect of escape, despair eventually settled on the six Fenians. The only relief from their sentence that they could see was the release that death would bring. Until then they would have to endure a living death.

6

A Daring Escape

While the six Fenians were in despair, a seventh Fenian, John Boyle O'Reilly, was planning to escape. He had been sent to the work gang of Deputy Warder Henry Woodman. The warder liked O'Reilly and gave him the job of delivering letters to the port town of Bunbury. While delivering these letters, O'Reilly was alone for hours. This gave him the perfect opportunity to escape.

O'Reilly met an Irish priest, Father Patrick McCabe, who was building a church in Bunbury. McCabe had great sympathy for the Fenian prisoners and offered to help O'Reilly. McCabe planned to bribe the skipper of a whaling ship that docked in the port to take O'Reilly on board.

At Christmas 1868, O'Reilly got a letter telling him that his mother had died six months earlier. This greatly depressed the Fenian. One afternoon, on his way back from Bunbury, he wandered into the bush, determined to die.

Luckily, he was found by another prisoner and recovered from his ordeal. But Father McCabe now realised that he had to act quickly before O'Reilly wandered into the bush once more. He might not be so lucky to survive a second time.

In January 1869, while delivering letters, O'Reilly met a man named Maguire. He was a friend of Father McCabe's and informed O'Reilly that the priest had found a whaling skipper willing to take the Fenian on board. A date was set for O'Reilly to escape from the work camp. He would then meet Maguire, who would be waiting with horses to take him to the rendezvous.

After dark on the date in February set for his escape, O'Reilly stripped off his hated prison garb and dressed in civilian clothes supplied by Maguire. He slipped away from the work camp, careful not to arouse suspicion from the guards or the other convicts. As he crept into the bush, a man's voice hailed him.

O'Reilly endured a moment of terror as he recognised the man as a released convict. He realised that if the man raised the alarm the escape plan was doomed. He would be put in chains, taken back to Fremantle and placed in solitary confinement. There, his body and spirit already weakened, he would most likely die.

But the man did not sound the alarm. Instead, he merely wished O'Reilly good luck. With his heart hammering in his chest, and shaking with relief, O'Reilly thanked the ex-convict and headed off into the darkness.

He met Maguire and two other men with the horses. O'Reilly, a former Hussar, was a fine horseman and soon the four were riding hard toward a rendezvous point further along the coast. O'Reilly, free again for the first time in years, exulted in the ride.

Some Fenian sympathisers and a man who owned a boat were waiting. The latter was being paid to help in the escape attempt and it was hoped that he would not betray them. Quickly, the men launched the boat and soon were rowing away from the Australian shore. Behind them, the breaking waves glowed white in the darkness.

The plan was to row out into international waters where the whaler, *Vigilant*, would pick up O'Reilly. Father McCabe had paid the skipper, Captain Anthony Baker, to take the Fenian on board.

As dawn broke, the men on the boat scanned the ocean for sight of a sail. No such sail appeared. As the day passed, and the sun mercilessly beat down from a clear blue sky, despair settled on O'Reilly.

Eventually he had to accept that the *Vigilant* was not going to appear. Weary, hungry and thirsty, the men rowed back to shore. Now they had to be even more alert. The authorities would know by now that O'Reilly had escaped and would be searching for him. If they found him, not only would O'Reilly be returned to prison but the others would be imprisoned for helping him escape.

They reached the shore without mishap and dragged the boat up on to the beach. While O'Reilly hid in the bush, the others returned to their homes. Maguire went back to Bunbury to see what had happened to the *Vigilant*. All promised that they would return the following morning.

O'Reilly slept fitfully that night. He knew that police with trackers would be out searching for him. If they found him he would be shown no mercy. He was also aware that there were poisonous snakes in the bush. Another fear was that Maguire and the others might not return, or might betray him.

Dawn eventually broke over the Indian Ocean. The sun sparkled on the blue water and a welcome breeze blew off the ocean. But O'Reilly, a poet and writer, had little appreciation of the scene. He was still fearful that Maguire might not return, or that a search party would find him.

John Boyle O'Reilly and his helpers drag the boat back up on the beach.
HAYDEN JOHNSON, AGED 15

The *Catalpa* Adventure

He now heard men approaching and peered out to see Maguire and the others returning. As O'Reilly calmed his thumping heart, Maguire informed him that the *Vigilant* had left Bunbury. O'Reilly was now just hours from freedom.

Again they rowed out into the ocean and around noon spotted the whaler. In desperate haste, they rowed furiously toward her. They tried signalling her with a cloth tied to an oar. As they drew near, they shouted to attract the attention of any sailor who might be on the lookout for them.

But the *Vigilant* did not stop or signal back. Instead, she sailed on. In silence, O'Reilly and the men watched her until she became a speck on the horizon. Still silent, they rowed back to shore and hauled the boat up on to the beach once more. O'Reilly was in despair and Maguire took him into the bush where a sympathetic family would hide him. Maguire also assured him that Father McCabe would bribe another skipper to pick him up within a week or so.

O'Reilly feared that he would be found or betrayed. So if he were to escape, he would have to do so by himself. He now learned that an abandoned boat lay a short distance along the shoreline. He decided to row out in it and try to find the *Vigilant*.

First, O'Reilly had to repair the boat. With this done, he set off one evening for the open ocean. He rowed all night, while sharks circled his boat. Dawn found him alone on the ocean. There was no shade and the pitiless sun beat down. Thirst plagued him. He became delirious, wearied by the rowing and the heat.

Then on the horizon he spotted a white shape against the blue sky. Shading his eyes he watched it. Could it be a sail? Or was he only imagining it? Slowly the shape grew larger. It was a sail! There was a ship out there!

A Daring Escape

O'Reilly's fatigue fell from him. Hope was at hand. Grabbing the oars, he began to row with all his might toward the ship. As he drew near, he could not believe his eyes. The ship was the *Vigilant* and she was heading toward him. He could see the sailors on board and hear them talking. He was saved!

Then, without warning, the *Vigilant* swung away. For a moment, O'Reilly could not believe his eyes. Then, bending his aching back he began to row with as much vigour as he could muster. But the whaler, with its sails billowing in the wind, quickly drew away from him. As the afternoon waned, he lost sight of the ship. Later, as darkness descended, he knew that all hope was gone.

Utterly in despair, O'Reilly rowed back to shore. By now he was broken in body and spirit. He reached the safety of the shore and, after hiding the boat, retreated into the bush where he collapsed, exhausted.

Days later, Maguire found him with some good news. Father McCabe had bribed the skipper of the whaler *Gazelle* to take O'Reilly on board. Tomorrow they would row out to meet the ship. O'Reilly's spirits lifted. Once more he had hope.

But there was a problem. A released convict named Henderson had learned of O'Reilly's escape plan. He was a nasty, brutish man and intended to escape with the Fenian. If he were not allowed to escape, he would inform the police of the plan. Though he was unhappy with this, O'Reilly had no choice but to agree.

Next morning, O'Reilly and the others rowed out to sea once more. Later that day they spotted the *Gazelle* and rowed toward her. O'Reilly knew that this was his last chance to escape.

But as dusk fell they still had not reached the whaler. She seemed to be sailing away from them. The men in the boat grew silent. O'Reilly's shoulders slumped, the first sign of the man's hopelessness. Even in the dusk, the other men could see the despair on his face.

Suddenly, without warning, the whaler came about. She headed right toward them. Those in the rowing boat cheered as ship drew near. In the near darkness they heard a voice call out, 'Hey there, O'Reilly?' The men cheered again as the *Gazelle* heaved to.

A rope ladder was thrown down. O'Reilly shook hands with Maguire and the men who had risked their freedom to help him escape. Then, gripping the rungs of the ladder and belying his exhaustion, he scrambled upwards where sailors helped him board the whaler.

Captain Gifford, the *Gazelle*'s skipper, welcomed O'Reilly on board. The captain already knew about the presence of Henderson and that he would have to take the convict. He could not risk leaving Henderson behind to betray them.

If Henderson told the authorities what had happened, they would send a British warship to find the *Gazelle*. Then both O'Reilly and Gifford, along with those who had helped in the escape, would end up in Fremantle Prison.

Gifford allowed Henderson on board, intending to put him ashore at their next port of call. The ladder was pulled up and the *Gazelle* prepared to get under sail once more. From the ship's deck, O'Reilly bid a farewell to Maguire and the men who had risked their freedom for him. Then, with a flap of a tautening sail and the creak of the ship's timbers, the *Gazelle* swung about and headed out to sea.

A Daring Escape

O'Reilly stood by the ship's guardrail and stared back toward the Australian shoreline, no longer visible in the darkness. While he revelled in his own freedom, he was saddened as he thought of his comrades who still languished in prison. They were weakening day by day fsrom hunger and overwork. If they were not rescued, they would soon die.

Standing in the darkness, O'Reilly vowed that when he reached America he would help in any attempt to rescue those men. He owed that much to his comrades who, like him, had willingly risked their lives so that Ireland might be free.

While he stood there, a sailor approached him and shook his hand. His name was Henry C. Hathaway. As the two men chatted in the darkness, they did not know that both of them would one day be involved in the rescue of the six Fenian prisoners from Fremantle Prison.

It was to be a rescue more dangerous and exciting than the escape of O'Reilly. It was a rescue that was to become part of folklore, known forever afterwards by the name of the ship involved, the whaler *Catalpa*.

7
Letter From a Tomb

When John Boyle O'Reilly reached America he wrote to Father McCabe. The priest passed on the news to the six Fenians still in prison. It buoyed up their spirits. If O'Reilly could escape, maybe they could too.

In 1870, William Gladstone, the British Prime Minister, ordered that the civilian Fenian prisoners be released. This was on the condition that they did not return to Ireland or Britain. But he made no such order concerning the six soldiers. This was because the Commander-in-Chief of the British army, the Duke of Cambridge, was opposed to their release. In his eyes, they had betrayed the army and if they were released, it would set a bad example to other soldiers.

Naturally, the news devastated the six Fenians. It left them without any hope. Now Thomas Hassett wrote a letter to O'Reilly, which was smuggled out of the prison by Father McCabe. In the letter, Hassett wrote of his hope of one day being free.

The letter reminded O'Reilly of the promise he had made that night while standing on the deck of the *Gazelle* as he sailed to freedom. Something had to be done to free the six Fenians. But what could be done? O'Reilly didn't know.

Letter From a Tomb

Meanwhile, Hassett could bear prison life no longer. He became determined to escape on a whaler, as O'Reilly had, or die in the attempt. One evening, Hassett slipped away from his work gang and eventually reached Bunbury. Here, a family hid him while Father McCabe tried to find a ship's captain willing to take the Fenian. But the money to bribe a skipper could not be raised.

After hiding for months, Hassett sneaked on board a ship, the *Southern Belle*. Once on board, he hid under tarpaulins. But since O'Reilly's escape the water police regularly searched ships leaving Bunbury.

Now, heavily armed, they boarded the *Southern Belle*. As the searchers drew near his hiding place, Hassett knew that they would find him. Fearing they would kill him and aware that his escape attempt was doomed, he gave himself up.

He was clapped in chains and taken to Bunbury Jail. Later, he was tried for trying to escape and sentenced to six months' solitary confinement. When he had served his sentence he was sent to one of the most notorious work gangs in the state. This punishment was virtually a death sentence.

Martin Hogan now wrote another letter, which eventually reached America. In it he wrote of his ordeal, and of the ordeal of his fellow Fenians. He begged those Fenians who now enjoyed their freedom to help him and his fellow prisoners escape.

This letter found its way into the hands of John Devoy. He knew Hogan and the other Fenian soldiers. Devoy had served time in Millbank Prison in England and knew what prison life was like. He had been released under Gladstone's orders and had gone to America, where he worked as a journalist.

Devoy was a member of the Fenian Brotherhood, which was

now named Clan na Gael. He decided that the organisation should attempt to rescue the six Fenian soldiers still in Fremantle Prison.

Devoy wanted to give the prisoners some hope. He wrote them a letter in which he promised to do what he could to help them. But his pleas to Clan na Gael for help in any rescue went unanswered. Their aim was to organise a rebellion in Ireland. They could not allow the fate of Fenian prisoners in Australia to interfere with that.

More letters came from the prisoners. In them they described the terrible conditions in prison and in the work gangs. One Fenian prisoner, Patrick Keating, who had been transported with them on the *Hougoumont*, was seriously ill. Overworked and undernourished, his heart had been weakened and he was on the verge of death.

O'Reilly, too, urged Clan na Gael to help the prisoners. But still no help was forthcoming. Then in the summer of 1874 a letter arrived in America from James Wilson, which was to become known as 'the letter from the tomb'. In it, Wilson pointed out that he and his comrades had been in Fremantle Prison for seven years. If they weren't rescued soon, they would die. The prison would indeed be their tomb.

Devoy was very moved by this letter. He became more determined than ever to help the men. Aware of O'Reilly's escape, he believed that it was possible to free the men. But to do so, he needed Clan na Gael's help.

In July 1874, Clan na Gael held a convention in Baltimore. With Hogan and Wilson's letters in his pocket, Devoy took the train there. In a speech to the delegates he spoke with passion about the need for a rescue attempt. His plan was to send a ship carrying armed Fenians to Western Australia to rescue the prisoners.

At first, the delegates listened politely, but remained unmoved. But when Devoy read Martin Hogan's letter, his audience was stunned into silence. After Devoy's speech a vote was taken. Such was the power of Devoy's words, and the impact of the letter, that the delegates voted for a rescue to be attempted.

An Australian Prisoners Rescue Committee was now set up with Devoy as its head. Among those appointed to the committee were James Reynolds and John W. Goff. Reynolds, who would play an important part in the rescue plan, was to become known by the nickname 'Catalpa Jim'.

In order for the plan to succeed two things were necessary. One was money. The other was secrecy. If any hint of the plan reached the British authorities, they would take action to ensure its failure.

Devoy circulated the Hogan and Wilson letters to all Clan na Gael branches in America. They had an immediate effect. Money poured into the rescue fund. Despite the opposition of some branches, $7,000 dollars was raised. It wasn't sufficient to put the plan into action, but it gave the committee great encouragement.

Devoy now travelled to Boston to discuss a rescue plan with O'Reilly. The latter's suggestion was that the committee should buy a whaling ship and hire a man from New Bedford, a whaling port near Boston, to sail it to Bunbury. The prisoners could make their way out to the ship, as he had done, and sail to freedom. O'Reilly strongly emphasised the need for secrecy. If an informer learned of the rescue attempt and informed the British, then it would be doomed to failure.

Neither Devoy nor O'Reilly knew the sailing people of

New Bedford. But O'Reilly knew a man who did. This was Henry C. Hathaway, who had stood by the rail of the *Gazelle* that night O'Reilly sailed to freedom. Now O'Reilly gave Devoy a letter of introduction to Hathaway.

As Devoy left O'Reilly in Boston that day, he could not know that luck was on his side. O'Reilly had actually given him the name of the best man in New Bedford to help him with his daring rescue plan.

8

A Rescue is Planned

Devoy took a train to New Bedford where he had his first sight of the port, which would play such an important part in his plan. The harbour was choked with ships, their tall masts pointing to the sky. Sailors and shore workers thronged the docksides. Smells of ozone and fish and whale oil hung in the air.

Devoy took it all in before making his way to his destination, which was the New Bedford Police Station. Henry C. Hathaway, the man he was to meet, was the station's Chief of the Night Police. When Hathaway saw O'Reilly's letter, he warmly welcomed Devoy.

Despite having sworn to uphold law and order, Hathaway was willing to help Devoy. He had learned about the Fenian prisoners from O'Reilly and did not regard them as criminals. He saw them as honourable men who were in prison because they had wanted freedom for Ireland. It was a cause Hathaway could identify with.

Hathaway now listened while Devoy outlined his plan. This was to buy a whaler, sail her to Western Australia and rescue the prisoners. Hathaway nodded in agreement from time to time, but did not speak. Afterwards, he gave his opinion of the plan, stating that it was capable of success.

If a whaler could be bought, she could sail to Australia. On the way, she could go whaling and the whale oil obtained on the journey could then be sold to help pay for the venture.

The men parted on good terms and promised to meet again to discuss the plan further. Devoy now wrote to some of those on the committee explaining that the plan could work and that he had found a man who could help them organise it.

Devoy and Hathaway met regularly over the next few weeks. They discussed the plan in great detail. The first step was to buy a suitable ship. Then they would have to find a good man to skipper her.

They decided that the plan would cost about $12,000. The rescue committee had about $7,000. Devoy thought that he could personally raise another $2,000. That left a balance of $3,000. More fund-raising would be required.

Meanwhile they needed a man to locate a suitable ship and purchase it. This man would have to deal with the paperwork involved in buying a ship and registering her. Hathaway had just such a man in mind. He was John T. Richardson, a noted New Bedford whaling agent. Now Hathaway arranged for Devoy to meet Richardson.

Richardson was a Quaker and had no ties to Ireland or her cause. But like Hathaway, who also had no Irish links, he respected Devoy and his cause. Perhaps because of his Quaker background, he saw the injustice in the imprisonment of the Fenians and in the harsh and brutal conditions under which they were held.

Richardson agreed to purchase a suitable whaling ship. He would make all the necessary arrangements to fit her out for the voyage and deal with the paperwork. He assured Devoy that he would do so with the utmost secrecy.

Now they had to find a skipper for the whaler. He would have to have exceptional qualities. Not only would he have to be capable of commanding a whaler, but would have to be willing to carry out the rescue mission. Such a mission could cost him his freedom, or even his life. As well as this, he would have to be a man who could keep a secret.

Richardson knew the ideal man for the job. He was George Smith Anthony and he was married to Richardson's daughter, Emma. He was now thirty-one years old and had been at sea since he was a boy. Not only was he a highly experienced whaling man, but he was trustworthy and would not betray the mission.

Devoy agreed to meet Anthony to see if he was suitable. The two men met one night at Richardson's premises in New Bedford in February 1875. Also at that meeting were James Reynolds and Henry Hathaway.

In Richardson's locked and darkened office, the five met. Before the meeting proper began, Devoy asked Anthony to give him his word that he would never speak of the meeting to anyone. It was a strange request, but Anthony trusted his father-in-law, and gave his word.

Devoy now outlined the plight of the Fenian prisoners in Australia. They were not criminals or convicts, he explained, but brave soldiers, whose only 'crime' was their desire to free their country from oppression. For this 'crime' they had been treated far worse than murderers and thieves. Now, if they were not rescued, they faced certain death in one of the most notorious convict colonies in the whole world.

Next, Devoy outlined the plan to rescue the imprisoned men. Then he came to the point of the meeting. 'Would you be willing to skipper such a vessel, Captain Anthony?' he asked. 'Would you undertake such a daring and dangerous mission?'

Anthony sat stunned. For a few moments he could not speak. His mind was in turmoil. Devoy had mentioned danger, but he could not have had any real idea of the dangers that would be involved in such a mission.

First of all there were the dangers associated with whaling. It was a job fraught with peril. But to sail to Western Australia and pick up six escaped prisoners posed even greater dangers. To men like Devoy, the Fenian prisoners were heroes and patriots. But to the British authorities, they were the worst kind of criminals, traitors to queen and empire.

Any ship taking on the prisoners would be regarded as an enemy of Britain. It would be liable to attack by British warships. Anthony knew that the British navy was the most powerful navy in the world. A whaler would stand little chance against the powerful British guns.

She could also face a threat from the American navy. If the American government learned of the rescue attempt, they would detain the whaler and her crew. Her captain could face charges of committing an act of war against another country, and face imprisonment.

Still, the prospect of adventure stirred Anthony's spirit. Since the age of fifteen he had served on whaling ships, rising to command the whaler *Hope On*. But after his marriage, Anthony had promised his wife that he would not go to sea again. He now worked as an engineer, but was bored with the job.

Every day he saw ships setting sail from the harbour. His

heart yearned to be on a ship once more, with the crack of her canvas and the groan of her timbers in his ears. Here was an opportunity to have that dream fulfilled. Here was an opportunity of a last great adventure.

The idea of a daring rescue also appealed to Anthony. Like the other men in the room he, too, disliked injustice. He knew that if a rescue attempt did not go ahead, then the prisoners in Australia would die there in chains. To a free spirit like Anthony, that was a terrible prospect to contemplate.

Yet he now had a wife and a daughter to consider. There was also his promise to Emma to bear in mind. He turned to Devoy and the other men. 'I need time to think about this,' he said. 'Can you give me that time?'

Devoy nodded. 'I can give you twenty-four hours,' he said. 'By then you must have made your decision.'

That night Anthony hardly slept as he considered the proposition. The next day at work he weighed up the dangers against the prospect of being in command of his own ship once more. Though he would be well paid for undertaking the mission, this was not an important consideration. He had already begun to feel a great sympathy for the prisoners and had a genuine desire to free them.

That evening after dinner, Anthony returned to Richardson's office. Devoy and the other men were already there. They were tense as they waited for Anthony's decision. Devoy had already concluded that Anthony was the ideal man for the job. If he refused to undertake the mission, it would be dealt a huge setback, one that might jeopardise the whole plan.

Anthony entered the office to complete silence. A single oil lamp cast dark shadows. The faces of Devoy and the others were pale blurs in the near darkness. For a moment no one spoke. Then Devoy asked the vital question. 'Captain Anthony,' he said quietly, 'will you undertake this mission?'

There was a moment's hesitation. Then in a firm voice Anthony spoke. 'Yes,' he said. 'I agree to undertake your mission.'

There were sighs of relief all round. The men shook hands, faces beaming in the flickering light. Then they sat to discuss the plan. Devoy instructed Richardson and Anthony to find a suitable ship and purchase her and have her fitted out for the voyage. When that was done, Anthony could hire a whaling crew and set out for Western Australia.

After the meeting, Anthony walked down to the harbour. It was dark now and there were few people about. The gulls, which usually wheeled among the masts, had gone to roost for the night. Anthony listened to the water lapping against the quay and the wind whistling in the ships' rigging.

One day soon he would come here and board his own vessel once more. He would give the command to cast off. Once clear of the harbour, he would order the sails to be hoisted. Then with his rolling ship beneath him, he would set off on what would be the last and greatest and most dangerous voyage of his life.

9
The *Catalpa* Weighs Anchor

Over the next few weeks Anthony and Richardson looked for a suitable ship without success. By March, Richardson was becoming worried. The whaling season began in May and soon ships would become more expensive.

Then Richardson received news that a suitable ship was being sold in Boston. She was the *Catalpa*. Richardson knew the ship and also knew that she would be ideal if she were seaworthy.

Richardson and Anthony travelled by train to Boston to inspect the *Catalpa*. She was built as a whaling ship in 1844 and weighed 202 tons. She was 30 metres long, 8 metres wide and 4 metres deep and operated as a converted merchantman.

After a thorough inspection, both men deemed her ideal for a long whaling voyage. Her masts and rigging were in good condition, as were her timbers. There was also room on board to build extra accommodation for the rescued prisoners.

Richardson now contacted Devoy. 'We have found an ideal ship,' he said. 'She is for sale at the bargain price of $5,250. I urge you to buy her immediately.'

Devoy was unable to secure sufficient funds immediately and Richardson put $4,000 of his own money toward the purchase of the *Catalpa*. To cover this debt, James Reynolds offered his own house as collateral.

Devoy and O'Reilly now asked an expert American naval officer, Lieutenant Tobin, to inspect the *Catalpa*. Tobin deemed the ship seaworthy. 'You got a bargain at that price,' he told the two men. It seemed that their luck was holding.

Henry Hathaway also travelled to Boston to inspect the *Catalpa*. He, too, was impressed with the ship and wrote to Devoy to say that she was a real bargain. In case the letter should fall into the wrong hands, Hathaway referred to the ship as a horse.

Once the *Catalpa* was purchased, she was taken to New Bedford for fitting out. Around the middle of March Captain Anthony stood on the deck of his new command, while a tugboat towed the *Catalpa* out of Boston Harbour. On the open sea Anthony felt the thrill of a rolling ship beneath him once more. Now he knew that, despite his wife Emma's protestations, he had made the correct decision.

The next day the *Catalpa* arrived in New Bedford Harbour where she was tied up at the wharf. Now one of New Bedford's finest shipwrights, John W. Howland was hired to convert her to a whaling ship again. Under the watchful eye of Captain Anthony, this work commenced.

A blubber deck was installed along with a furnace and hoists and pulleys for hauling whales on board. The hull was fitted with new copper. Small whaling boats for hunting whales were bought and fitted on the decks. Cabins were rearranged and other repairs carried out.

Casks for storing whale oil and water were purchased. Harpoons and bomb-lances, needed for whaling, were also bought. Other essentials for a long voyage like food and medicines were stored on board.

The *Catalpa* Weighs Anchor

One of the important items Anthony purchased was a ship's chronometer. It would be used on the voyage to work out the *Catalpa*'s exact position. This was vital if the voyage was to progress without serious mishap. Later, this chronometer would cause Anthony much trouble.

The cost of fitting out and provisioning the ship proved more costly than had been estimated. The total cost came close to $19,000. This put a burden on Devoy, who had to try and find the extra money. He now approached various Clan na Gael branches seeking funds. Many refused to help but others did give money.

Eventually the ship was ready to sail. Captain Anthony now set about hiring a crew. These ordinary crewmen were from Malaya, Singapore, the Cape Verde Islands and the Azores. He also needed a First Mate and Anthony knew just the man he wanted. This was Samuel Smith, a highly experienced whaling man.

Anthony went to see Smith and offered him the position of First Mate. He did not tell Smith the real reason for the voyage. Smith was engaged to be married, and at first was unwilling to accept the position. But when offered excellent wages and a portion of any profit, Smith accepted the position of First Mate on the *Catalpa*.

Anthony was delighted with his good luck. He knew he would need a good man to help him handle any problems that might arise with the crew. Whaling men were tough and resilient. They were not men who could be easily cowed or forced to do anything against their will.

None of the crew would be told of the real purpose of the voyage. Anthony would keep that to himself until they were near Australia. When he did tell them, he could not predict how they would react to having been deceived and exposed to grave danger. Although Anthony, as the ship's captain, would be held responsible by the British authorities if the ship were captured, the crew might still end up in prison as accessories to criminal activity.

When the time came to inform the crew of the real purpose of the voyage, Anthony wanted a good man on his side. He knew that Sam Smith was that man and now felt a lot happier that he had this experienced, reliable sailor as First Mate.

But a problem arose when Clan na Gael insisted that some of its members should also go on the voyage. As they had provided the finance, Devoy had to accept this condition. At first it was decided to send four men. But Devoy realised that this could imperil the whole plan. If the British authorities learned that four Irishmen were on board a whaler bound for the Southern Ocean, they might figure out the reason for them going there.

Eventually it was decided that two men would go. One was Dennis Duggan, who would be the ship's carpenter. The other was Thomas Brennan. The latter was quick-tempered and neither Devoy nor Captain Anthony wanted him on the *Catalpa*. Eventually, a compromise was reached. Brennan would sail on another whaler to the Azores and Anthony would pick him up there.

By the end of April 1875 all was ready. On Thursday 29 April 1875, Captain Anthony said goodbye to his wife and daughter before making his way to the harbour. Here he met with Devoy, Hathaway, Richardson and other members of the Rescue Committee. Anthony's friends had also come to bid him farewell and wish him luck.

Anthony went on board along with Devoy and the other men who had been involved in the venture. Anthony gave the order for the mooring lines to be cast off and a tugboat towed the *Catalpa* out into Buzzards Bay. As was the custom, the onlookers called out their best wishes for a successful voyage.

The men from the Rescue Committee now had dinner with Captain Anthony. Then they descended to a whaleboat and rowed back to New Bedford. On board the *Catalpa*, Captain Anthony gave the order: 'Hoist the sails.' Sailors clambered into the rigging and unfurled the sails. Slowly, the *Catalpa* headed out to sea.

The Catalpa *being towed out into Buzzards Bay by a tugboat.*
BARBARA CASEY, AGED 12

The *Catalpa* Adventure

Captain Anthony stood on the deck, his legs braced against the rolling of the ship. Above his head the sails flapped and cracked in the stiffening breeze. The ship's timbers creaked as she ploughed through the waves, which gradually got longer and higher as the *Catalpa* reached open water.

Beyond lay nearly 30,000 kilometres of ocean, some of it the most dangerous on earth. Even if they survived such a long and perilous voyage, an even greater danger awaited them when they reached their destination.

Anthony was setting out on a voyage to rescue men he had never known. If anything went wrong in Australia he could end up in prison with the men he intended rescuing. Echoing the words of James Wilson, which had been partly responsible for this voyage, Fremantle Prison might not only become his prison, but also his tomb.

Captain Anthony turned to take a last look at New Bedford. There, he had recently bid goodbye to his wife and daughter. He had also bid goodbye to his mother who, for the past few days, had been gravely ill. As he looked back at the port, he was aware that he might never see his loved ones again.

10

The Plot Unfolds

E ven as the Catalpa set sail, word had already reached the British authorities that a rescue attempt was being planned. But no one on the British side imagined that Clan na Gael would organise the kind of breakout that was now under way. Instead, they suspected that any rescue attempt would be similar to that of O'Reilly's, with a whaling skipper being bribed to take the prisoners on his ship.

As a result of this, the water police in Bunbury kept a vigilant eye on all whaling ships anchored there. The authorities had been severely embarrassed by O'Reilly's escape and were determined that there would be no repeat.

A Detective Thomas Rowe warned the authorities in Fremantle of the possibility of a rescue attempt. But the authorities did not heed his warnings. Instead, they had relaxed the conditions under which the six Fenians were being held. They were no longer with the work gangs but involved in less demanding duties.

This situation had arisen because the prisoners were suffering the effects of their years of imprisonment. They were weak and malnourished, and no longer capable of working under the brutal conditions of a work gang. Sometimes their work duties took them outside the prison, where they were often alone and unguarded. This gave them an ideal opportunity to escape.

Meanwhile, in America, the Rescue Committee had to decide on who should go to Australia to help with the rescue. At first, Devoy proposed that he should go. But the members rejected this. If such a high profile figure arrived in Australia, the authorities might suspect his purpose for being there.

Devoy then proposed that the best man to send there was John J. Breslin. Ironically, Breslin had once been Superintendent of Richmond Prison in Dublin. In this capacity, he had helped in the escape of James Stephens. After the escape, he had fled to America.

Breslin was a tall, powerfully built man. He was intelligent and resourceful and had a great love of Ireland. The Rescue Committee accepted him and Devoy now met Breslin and explained the plan to him. Right from the beginning, Breslin knew the dangers involved. But he was a courageous man and the idea of rescuing the Fenian prisoners appealed to him. 'I'll go to Australia,' he told Devoy without any hesitation.

A second man would be needed to help Breslin. The Californian branch of Clan na Gael recommended a Corkman, Thomas Desmond. He was a fervent Fenian who had fought bravely in the American Civil War. At present he was a sheriff in San Francisco, and was deemed ideal for the job.

With the matter settled, Breslin left New York for California. Here, he met Desmond, whom he liked right from the start. They decided that they could not risk using their own names so chose new ones.

Breslin called himself James Collins. He would pretend to be a wealthy American who wished to speculate in gold and land in Western Australia. Desmond would be known as Tom Johnson, a carriage maker, which was his trade. Once they embarked on the venture, they would pretend to be strangers.

Breslin set about finding out all he could about Fremantle and the prison and about Bunbury. He also sought the names of those living there who were sympathetic to the Fenian cause and might be willing to help with the rescue.

Breslin was given several thousand dollars to help carry off the pretence of being a wealthy businessman. He was also supplied with a dummy bank draft for a large sum of money. With this, he could keep up the pretence of being a wealthy man who wished to buy land or gold mining rights.

Breslin now booked two passages on board a ship, the *Cyphranes*, bound for Sydney in Australia. In September 1875, Breslin and Desmond boarded the ship in San Francisco docks. Breslin, as befitting a wealthy man, travelled First Class. Desmond, the working man, travelled Second Class.

Both men stood by the ship's rail as the *Cyphranes* slipped her moorings and headed out into the Pacific Ocean. Like the men on the *Catalpa*, they too were bound for Australia, not knowing if they would ever see America again. Both had been chosen for their courage and determination. These were the very qualities that they would soon need if their mission was to succeed.

Would they succeed in freeing the six Fenian prisoners? Would they then rendezvous with Captain Anthony and the *Catalpa* and sail to freedom? Or would they end up in Fremantle Prison and die there? If either man felt any fear at this prospect, he did not show it.

The success or failure of the plan now rested on three men: Captain Anthony, John J. Breslin and Tom Desmond. All three were brave and loyal and would honour their word. If any men could succeed in rescuing the six prisoners, these were the men. Devoy and Clan na Gael had chosen well. Now all they and the prisoners in Fremantle Prison could do was wait and hope.

11

A Terrible Accident

The *Catalpa* sailed to the south Atlantic, one of the best whaling areas in the world. Here, Anthony intended to hunt whales so as not to arouse the suspicions of the crew. If they suspected that they had been deceived, they might mutiny or desert the ship at the first opportunity.

Anthony, too, did not want to arouse any suspicion in his First Mate, Smith. He was a shrewd man and, if they did not go whaling, he would know something was amiss. Anthony needed Smith. Without him, he could not go ahead with the plan.

Funding for the venture was to be supplemented with money obtained from the sale of the whale oil. So it was imperative that they catch whales. If they didn't do so, their pay would be greatly diminished.

Today, people consider hunting whales to be cruel and many countries have banned whaling. Another reason for the ban is that some species of whale are in danger of extinction from hunting. But 150 years ago, whale oil was a vital product and so whaling was an important industry. Now that we have replaced whale oil with mineral oil, we no longer need to hunt whales as was the case at the time of the *Catalpa* rescue.

As the *Catalpa* reached the whaling grounds, the crew made ready the 10-metre-long whaling boats. Then in early May whales were spotted. The whaling boats were lowered and a hunt began. It was a promising start, with one whale taken. The crew, pleased with the success, worked enthusiastically cutting up the carcass and boiling the blubber to make oil.

More whales were caught in the following days. Though the crew worked long hours boiling up the blubber and filling casks with oil, they were in a positive mood. But their jubilation was short lived. Over the next weeks the *Catalpa* failed to find any more whales.

Then, when morale was at its lowest, a whale was sighted. As it blew water high into the air, a lookout shouted: 'Thar she blows!' Hearing the age-old warning cry of a whaling man, the crew cheered.

The whaling boats were lowered and the chase began. It was back-breaking work rowing a whaleboat, but with success in sight, the men bent to the oars. The small boats sped across the waves in pursuit of the great creature.

Slowly but surely they gained on the whale. Soon they were near enough for Smith to fire a harpoon. It struck the whale, sending the mammal into a frenzy. With sweeps of its mighty tail, it surged forward, dragging the whaleboat behind it.

This was a dangerous time for the whalers as their small boat could be swamped. It could also capsize, throwing the men into the water. Most whaling men could not swim. So if they ended up in the water they were likely to drown before they could be rescued.

The whale pulled the boat for what seemed ages before exhaustion and its injury slowed it down. Now the whaleboat was able to draw near to the creature. This gave Sam Smith the opportunity to kill it with his lance. But as Smith drove the

'Thar she blows!'
GRAEME BOURKE, AGED 15

lance into the stricken whale, it lashed its massive tail in its death throes.

The tail struck Smith and knocked him out of the boat. As he fell into the water, a more deadly danger than drowning threatened his life. Sharks, drawn to the scene by the smell of blood, drew near.

Fins sliced through the water, which was seething red from the whale's blood.

Ominously, the sharks closed in for the kill. Frantically, the men on the whaleboat manoeuvred it close to Smith, who was unconscious. Hands grabbed him and hauled him into the boat with only seconds to spare. As the sharks tore at the whale's carcass, the shocked sailors rowed back to the *Catalpa*.

As Smith was hauled on board, Anthony looked on anxiously. He was aware that if Smith was seriously injured he could die. In that event, the rescue would have to be abandoned. Anthony could not consider going on to Australia without the man he had hand-picked to assist him.

Smith was still unconscious and bleeding from deep gashes to his head. He was taken to his cabin where his wounds were cleaned and dressed. Now all Anthony could do was wait and hope.

A sense of gloom descended on the crew. Sailors, and especially whaling men, were very superstitious. An incident like this was regarded as an ill omen. So it was with a lack of enthusiasm that they hauled in the whale's carcass, already badly torn by the sharks.

Smith remained unconscious that night. Then, to everyone's relief, not least of all Captain Anthony, he regained consciousness the next morning. Though weak from loss of blood, the First

A Terrible Accident

Mate insisted on supervising the cutting up and boiling of the whale that had almost caused his death.

By October, the *Catalpa* reached the island of Flores in the Azores. She anchored here and took on board fresh supplies. Then she set sail once more, bound for the Portuguese island of Fayal.

At the end of October, Anthony glimpsed the massive fortress at Fayal. The *Catalpa* docked and the casks of whale oil were unloaded. Fresh supplies of food and water were brought on board and essential repairs carried out. Anthony also bought a chronometer from the captain of another whaling vessel, having found that his own one was faulty.

But then a problem arose, which could threaten the venture. A sailor named Bolles deserted and persuaded a number of other men to desert with him. Three crewmen had already left the ship owing to illness. This left Anthony with too small a crew to sail the *Catalpa* to Australia.

He had only one choice open to him. That was to illegally recruit men wishing to escape from Fayal. These were men who did not have passports, or who were in trouble with the authorities, or who were criminals. It was a serious offence to recruit such men and Anthony was risking his freedom and reputation in so doing. But he had no other choice.

These men could not openly go aboard the *Catalpa* while she was in the harbour. They had to be picked up at night from a secluded cove. While a boat was taking the men to the *Catalpa*, a Portuguese patrol boat arrived on the scene. For a moment all seemed lost. But luckily the patrol boat did not interfere and the men safely reached the ship.

Anthony, aware that his luck might run out, decided to sail right away. He had another good reason for doing so. News had reached him that Thomas Brennan was about to arrive in Fayal to join the *Catalpa*. Anthony still did not wish to have him on board and was anxious to get away before Brennan arrived.

Anthony ordered that the anchors be raised and the mooring lines cast off. The sails were unfurled to catch the breeze and the *Catalpa* sailed from Fayal without Brennan. She was bound for the island of Tenerife, her last stop before she set out for Western Australia.

Anthony knew that it was time to take Sam Smith into his confidence. Smith had recovered from his injuries and was his old self again. But how would he react when he learned that he had been deceived? Would he be willing to go ahead with the rescue when made aware of the risks involved? Anthony did not know. But he would soon find out. He intended to tell Smith everything before they reached Tenerife.

12

Catalpa Under Arrest

An anxious Anthony summoned Smith to his cabin. Even as Smith entered the cabin, Anthony knew that his First Mate was already suspicious. Aware of this, he decided to come right to the point.

'I have not been honest with you,' Anthony began. 'I must tell you now that when we sail from Tenerife we will not be going whaling. We are sailing to Western Australia where we are going to rescue six Irish prisoners.'

Smith looked astonished. If he had tried to guess at the real purpose of the voyage then he had obviously been greatly mistaken. For a moment there was silence. As Smith had not yet reacted angrily to the news, Anthony hurried on.

'These six men are Irish patriots,' he told Smith. 'Their only crime is that they wished to free their country from British oppression. For that they were sentenced to penal servitude for life. They have been brutally treated, and if they are not rescued they will soon die.'

Still Smith did not speak. He stared at Anthony, as if he could not believe what he was hearing. 'The *Catalpa* has been purchased and equipped for one purpose only,' Anthony continued. 'That is to sail to Western Australia and rescue those six misfortunate men. We went whaling so as to hide the true purpose of our voyage, and to help pay for it.'

'I was asked to command this mission and I agreed. I felt it was my duty. I chose you as my First Mate because you are one of the finest whaling men I know. Now that you know the real purpose of this voyage, you are free to make up your own mind as to what you wish to do. Will you come with me to Australia or leave the *Catalpa* at Tenerife?'

To Anthony's surprise, Smith now responded immediately. 'I'm with you,' he said. 'I will sail with you to Australia.'

Anthony breathed a great sigh of relief and shook his First Mate's hand. He had chosen the right man for the venture. He now would be able to rely on Smith later when he informed the crew of their true purpose. If there was trouble, Anthony wanted a good man by his side. Now he knew that he had such a man.

In the third week of November 1875 the *Catalpa* reached Tenerife. Here, Anthony encountered trouble from an unexpected source. Officials boarded the ship and demanded to see the ship's papers. As a result of the desertions, these now showed that there were three fewer men on board. There was also the problem that the new crewmen did not have passports or papers.

The officials informed Anthony that the *Catalpa* was 'under arrest'. They demanded all documents relating to the voyage, including she ship's log. Anthony had to hand them over. He knew that this was a very serious matter. He could be thrown in jail and accused of murdering the three missing seamen.

It was now that Anthony's character and bearing came to his aid. He went ashore and met the consul. He explained to him that some of his crew had deserted at Fayal and he'd had to sign on new men.

Catalpa Under Arrest

Anthony had brought with him the papers belonging to those who had deserted. Now he pretended that these papers belonged to the crewmen he had signed on. He invited the consul to come on board the *Catalpa* and check out the crew. Anthony's character impressed the consul and he agreed to this.

The consul, accompanied by a squad of soldiers, boarded the ship. Anthony looked on anxiously as the crew was inspected. If the consul questioned the crew too closely, or became suspicious, then all was lost. But the consul seemed satisfied and informed Anthony that the *Catalpa* was no longer 'under arrest'.

Utterly relieved, Anthony decided to sail at the first opportunity. Further stores and water were taken on board, as well as a supply of timber. This, Anthony informed the crew, was to be used for repairs. In reality it would be used by Duggan to build the extra accommodation that would be required for the six prisoners.

In the last week of November 1875, Anthony gave the order for the *Catalpa* to be made ready to sail. With great relief, he saw the coastline of Tenerife fall behind as the *Catalpa* eased out into the Atlantic. On the deck of a rolling ship, Anthony was where he felt most at home. With a warm breeze filling the sails and the sun's heat on his face, he should have been a contented man.

But Anthony now knew that he was on the final and most fraught part of the journey to Australia. They would not make land again until they reached Bunbury. He knew, too, that before then he would have to inform the crew of the real purpose of the voyage. If they mutinied, he and Smith and Duggan might not be able to hold the ship against them. If the crew took over the *Catalpa*, the three of them would never reach Australia. Instead they would find watery graves in the depths of the ocean, thousands of kilometres from homes and loved ones.

13
Plan in Jeopardy

In mid-October 1875, John J. Breslin and Tom Desmond arrived in Sydney. Here, they were shocked to discover that Fenians living in Australia were putting together a plan to rescue the six prisoners. Both men realised that this could jeopardise their own plan. They would have to do something urgently to sort out the problem.

Both men now met with two Fenian contacts in Sydney. One of these was a man named Kelly, who had served time in Fremantle Prison. He had suffered greatly there and was in bad health. The other man was named John King, a member of the IRB in Sydney.

These two men were equally shocked to learn of the *Catalpa* plan. As Breslin now outlined his plan, King and Kelly realised that it had the best chance of success. They agreed to abandon their own plan and to do whatever they could to assist Breslin and Desmond.

Both men now travelled separately to Melbourne where they booked a passage to Fremantle on a Royal Navy steamer, the *Georgette*. In mid-November they arrived in Fremantle. As the ship docked, both men were on deck to get their first glimpse of the fortress-like building that was Fremantle Prison.

Plan in Jeopardy

On the docks, half-starved men in the dreaded convict uniform of Drogheda linen toiled under the watchful eye of armed warders. If Breslin or Desmond had any doubts about their mission, the sight of these pitiful men quickly quelled them.

Both men disembarked separately. Breslin booked into the Emerald Isle Hotel while Desmond took a coach to Perth. There he would try to obtain work as a carriage builder or a stable hand. Either position would give him access to horses, which would be essential for the rescue.

Desmond quickly found a job building carriages. Meanwhile, Breslin set about creating the impression that he was a wealthy American businessman. He also decided to seek the help of Father McCabe, who had contact with the six men within the prison.

One Sunday, Breslin went to hear Mass said by Father McCabe in Fremantle church. There, he had his first glimpse of five of the prisoners. Darragh, not being a Catholic, did not attend Mass.

On that first Sunday, Breslin did not speak to Father McCabe. But later that week he bought new altar cloths and vestments for the church. On the next Sunday, Father McCabe thanked 'Mr Collins', the name by which Breslin was known, for his gifts. 'I'm afraid, Father,' Breslin said, 'that my name isn't Collins.'

Father McCabe was not surprised at this revelation. There were many men in Australia who used false names. Most were criminals trying to escape justice. Others were ticket-of-leave men. These were men who had been allowed out of prison on parole and had absconded. There were also Irishmen sympathetic to the cause of Irish freedom who used false names in order to avoid the authorities.

But this 'Mr Collins', or whatever his real name was, did not look like any of those men. The priest wondered who he really was and why he had divulged his secret to him. It seemed an odd thing to do.

John J. Breslin hesitated, then cleared his throat. 'I was sent here from America by people we both know,' he continued. 'One of them you once knew very well. His name is John Boyle O'Reilly.'

Father McCabe was stunned. What could this mean? What had brought this stranger to Fremantle? Could it possibly be . . .? The priest could not even begin to hope that his prayers might at last be answered. Would the five gaunt men he had seen in his church this very morning, dressed in the hated garb of a common convict, at last see the light of freedom?

The two men stared at each other. Then Breslin spoke. 'I'm John Breslin,' he said. 'I'm here on a mission to free the six Fenian prisoners from Fremantle Prison.'

At first Father McCabe was too overcome to speak. His prayers had been answered! When he recovered from the shock he grasped Breslin's hand. The name was familiar. Where had he heard it? Then the priest remembered. 'You're the man who rescued James Stephens,' he exclaimed.

Breslin nodded. 'I helped in that attempt,' he said modestly. 'Now I need your help to free our loyal patriots.'

Father McCabe was nodding. He had tears in his eyes. 'I will do whatever I can to help,' he said. 'Just tell me what you need.'

'We need to get word of the plan to the prisoners,' Breslin said. 'Can I rely on you to do that?'

'You can indeed,' Father McCabe said, still not recovered from the shock. He knew it would take time before he did so.

Plan in Jeopardy

He had waited so long for help to come, that now, when it had come, he was finding it difficult to believe.

Breslin now took a note from his pocket and handed it to the priest. 'You must get this note to one of the prisoners,' he said.

Father McCabe took the note. 'I'll see to it,' he assured Breslin.

'Thanks, Father,' Breslin said. 'And now I must tell you of this plan.'

Breslin now outlined the plan to the priest. With each revelation, Father McCabe shook his head in disbelief. Could what he was hearing be true? Was this all a dream and would he wake to reality and have to fight his despair? But then he realised that this was real. He and the prisoners had waited so long for hope that it was only natural that he should have doubts.

As he stared at John Breslin, the hero who had helped in James Stephens' daring escape, Father McCabe believed that the plan would succeed. One day soon the *Catalpa* would sail from Australia with the six Fenian prisoners on board. It would carry them all the way to America, the land of the free.

14

Where is the *Catalpa*?

Father McCabe passed Breslin's letter to a ticket-of-leave
Fenian named Foley. No longer confined to the prison,
Foley could move about freely. On his next visit to the
prison he secretly passed the letter to James Wilson.

Like Father McCabe, Wilson was stunned to learn of Breslin's
presence in Fremantle. At first he could hardly believe that help
was at hand and that there was now a possibility of escape.

Wilson destroyed the letter after reading it. Filled with
renewed hope, he told the other five Fenians the good news.
They, like Wilson, had waited so long for good news that at first
it was hard to accept.

'Can we really believe it?' they asked Wilson, who assured
them that they could. 'Be prepared for an escape attempt,' he told
them. 'But be very careful. Don't speak of this to anyone. We
must not change our habits or arouse suspicion.'

With refreshed optimism that soon they would be free, the
six Fenians continued as before. Darragh now worked as a clerk;
Wilson had a job in the prison stables and Hassett was a
gardener; Cranston helped out in the prison storehouse while
Hogan did odd jobs. Harrington worked on the docks. Now all
six men waited for further news.

Breslin was not idle and in the following weeks met many

of Fremantle's most prominent citizens. He met the governor of the province, Sir William Robinson, and was even given a tour of the prison by its superintendent, Joseph Doonan.

On the tour Breslin could see how secure the prison was and how difficult it would be for anyone to escape from within the walls. Somehow the prisoners would have to arrange to be outside the walls on the day of the rescue. If they couldn't get outside the walls, then the *Catalpa* would return to America without them.

He decided he would need to speak to at least one of the prisoners and again asked Father McCabe for help. The priest approached Superintendant Doonan, seeking a prisoner to drive him around the work camps in the province. By a stroke of luck, Doonan assigned James Wilson to the job.

An arrangement was now made for Breslin to meet Father McCabe and Wilson out in the bush. When the three men met Breslin could see immediately how prison life had aged Wilson. He looked more like an old man and was clearly in poor health.

After the two men shook hands, Breslin explained the plan to the gaunt Wilson. 'I have come to take you to America,' he told the prisoner. 'We have bought a ship and it will soon arrive here and take all six of you to freedom.'

Even yet Wilson found it hard to believe. But Breslin convinced him it was true and that the ship would soon arrive. 'You need to be ready when I give the word,' Breslin said. 'But it will be impossible for you to escape from inside the prison. So it's vital that you get work outside. Now don't speak to anyone, don't get in trouble and be ready when I give you the word.'

The men shook hands again and Wilson drove Father McCabe away. Breslin returned to Fremantle, aware that he had come just in time. If the other prisoners were as haggard and ill as Wilson, then they would not survive much longer.

Breslin and the prisoners could now only await the arrival of the *Catalpa*. In the following weeks, Breslin kept up his pretence as the wealthy American seeking investment opportunities. He travelled about the area and met with many prominent businessmen.

Meanwhile, a second part of the rescue plan was going well. Tom Desmond was now employed in Perth. As a carriage maker, he had contact with many of those who owned horses. He was satisfied that when the time came he would be able to borrow or hire or even steal horses and a carriage.

But January and February passed, and the *Catalpa* did not arrive in Bunbury. Breslin was still meeting secretly with Wilson, who was beginning to worry about the ship's non-arrival. He and the other prisoners were losing heart. They couldn't help but worry that even yet their hopes could be dashed. If this rescue attempt failed, they would not get another chance. They would all die here wearing the hated clothes of a convict, just as the brave Patrick Keating had died.

'You must have patience and courage,' Breslin told Wilson. 'The *Catalpa* will arrive. Captain Anthony is an honourable man. He will not let us down.'

But as weeks passed, and with no word from the *Catalpa*, Breslin began to worry. He had trusted Anthony implicitly, but was well aware that many things could go wrong during an ocean voyage. The ship might have run into a storm and sunk. The crew might have mutinied and murdered Anthony and Duggan. Or perhaps they had been delayed by bad weather. Whichever it might be, there was nothing they could do about it. All they could all do was wait and hope and pray.

15

An Extraordinary Meeting at Sea

At the beginning of 1876, British spies learned of a plot to free the Fenian prisoners in Fremantle. This information was passed to the governor of Western Australia. Aware of the embarrassment caused by O'Reilly's escape, the governor was determined that no prisoner would escape while he was in charge.

He informed his officials of this possible plot. But again, everyone assumed that an attempt would be made to bribe a whaling skipper to take the prisoners on board his ship. This led to a vigilant watch being kept on all whaling vessels docking in Bunbury. But such was the secrecy surrounding the *Catalpa* that no word of that plan leaked out.

While the water police watched the arrival and departure of the whalers, the *Catalpa* was still a long way from Bunbury. Slack winds had slowed her progress. A number of whales had also been caught and this, too, had delayed the ship.

As yet Anthony had not informed his crew of the real purpose of the voyage. He had only told them they were on their way to the River Plate whaling grounds off the South American coast. He planned to be close to Australia before he told them of their real purpose.

The wind shrieked in the rigging and monstrous waves struck the hull.
WOJTEK POKRYWCZYNSKI, AGED 13

An Extraordinary Meeting at Sea

In the second week of February the *Catalpa* almost met with disaster. Without warning, a storm blew up. Within an hour, the wind was shrieking in the rigging. Monstrous waves struck the hull, forcing the ship over on her side. If a second wave struck before she righted herself she would capsize. If that happened, the ship and all those on board would be doomed.

Captain Anthony was on deck as the storm struck. Above the howling and shrieking of the wind he shouted orders to his crew to reef the sails before they were ripped apart or the rigging torn down. He also worried that the masts might be broken.

Sails were torn and ripped from the rigging. Tattered canvas flapped wildly in the wind as the *Catalpa* rode out the storm.

Eventually the storm blew itself out and the danger passed. But now another problem faced Anthony. A ship, which was also in the area, approached the *Catalpa*. She was a whaler, the *Platina*, out of New Bedford. It was customary for ships' captains to stop and exchange news while at sea. Anthony had no choice but to heave to and greet the *Platina*.

He was aware that if her captain asked too many questions he might become suspicious of the reason for the voyage. If he then spoke of his suspicions to another captain bound for Bunbury, news might reach the port of the *Catalpa*'s real purpose. Anthony could sail into the port with soldiers waiting to arrest him.

Anthony knew the ship and her captain, Walter Howland, a relative of the shipwright, John Howland. Walter was a friend of Anthony's. But right now he was the last man Anthony wished to meet.

Anthony had his crew lower a whaleboat and row him over to the *Platina*. When he climbed on board, Howland greeted his old friend with a firm handshake and the question Anthony had been dreading: 'What are you doing in this part of the ocean?'

'I have permission to hunt whales wherever I wish,' Anthony replied. But this explanation did not allay Howland's suspicions. He continued to question Anthony who did his best to deflect the questions and quell the other man's suspicions.

But now another problem arose. Ships' crews also took the chance to exchange news and boast of the whales they had caught. As the whalers of the two ships chatted, the *Catalpa* crewmen learned that their ship was on course for Australia and New Zealand and not the River Plate.

This deception by Captain Anthony could have led to serious unrest among his crew. But in fact it worked to Anthony's benefit. His crew simply thought he had changed his mind and was going whaling in New Zealand waters. Anthony could now keep up this ruse as he sailed toward that part of the world.

Relieved at his fortune, Anthony bade goodbye to Howland and the *Catalpa* sailed on once more. A few days later Anthony spotted another ship. This was a British merchantman, the *Ocean Bounty*. Anthony again hove to and was rowed over to the ship.

A smiling Englishman welcomed him on board. After exchanging handshakes, the captain took Anthony to his cabin. Here he informed Anthony that he had made many voyages across the Indian Ocean. Then to Anthony's disbelief, the captain went onto say that he had commanded the last ship to bring convicts to Australia.

While Anthony tried to hide his shock, the man introduced himself. 'I'm Captain Cozens,' he said. 'I was captain of the convict ship, the *Hougoumont*. One of the convicts I transported, a Fenian named O'Reilly, later escaped on one of your whaling ships. I'm sure you know of that?'

An Extraordinary Meeting at Sea

Captain Anthony could only bluster and claim that he did not know of the man. All the while he couldn't help but stare at Cozens. What fates had conspired to have the man who had transported the six Fenians to Australia meet the man who was on his way there to rescue them?

Anthony realised that his whole mission was now in grave danger. If Cozens guessed at Anthony's real purpose, he would inform the authorities of the *Catalpa*'s intentions and the mission would have to be abandoned. Not only that, but British warships might hunt down the *Catalpa* and arrest Anthony. But to Anthony's great relief, Cozens did not appear suspicious.

It was obvious from Cozens' talk that he knew the Western Australian coastline very well. Anthony decided to ask the captain if he could look at some charts of the seas around there. Cozens was only too eager to help. 'Here,' he said, 'is the chart I had on board the *Hougoumont*. I don't think I'll need it again.' With that he laughed. 'You take it,' he said. 'I'm sure you'll make more use of it than I will.'

Anthony gratefully took the chart and thanked Captain Cozens. As he was rowed back to the *Catalpa* Anthony could not keep from smiling at Cozens' words. If only the captain knew what Anthony intended to do with the chart, he would not have been so generous.

With Anthony back on board, the *Catalpa* got under way once more. In his cabin, Anthony and Smith pored over the chart, both men smiling at the irony of it all. The very chart that had been used to bring the Fenian prisoners safely to Australia nine years before would now be used to free them. It was, Anthony thought, perfect poetic justice.

16

Are British Spies Watching?

In Fremantle, as January and February passed, John J. Breslin grew more anxious by the day. By March he was beginning to believe that something terrible had happened to the *Catalpa*, and that the mission was doomed to failure.

He was also running out of funds. Once his money was gone he would no longer be able to keep up his pretence of being a wealthy businessman. He wrote to America seeking more money and inquiring for news of the *Catalpa*. No money was sent to him, and no news of the *Catalpa* had reached New Bedford.

Those who knew about the venture began to wonder if Captain Anthony had betrayed them. Had he sailed away in the *Catalpa* with no intention of keeping his word? If he had done so, there was nothing they could do.

The prisoners, too, were beginning to despair. Breslin had promised that the *Catalpa* would reach Bunbury in January or early February. But as the weeks passed, the prisoners' spirits sank further.

They feared that the authorities would learn of the rescue attempt. If that happened, they would be sent to work camps out in the bush. Already weakened by years in prison, and suffering ill health, they knew this would kill them. In their hearts they knew that this was their only chance of being rescued. If it failed, they would never escape.

Breslin's money problem was solved when John King arrived in Fremantle with fresh funds. Breslin had also found an ideal spot from where the *Catalpa* could pick up the prisoners. This was at Rockingham beach, 32 kilometres from Fremantle. With horses, it could be reached in just over two hours. All was now ready, except there was still no sign of the ship.

Breslin, driven to distraction with anxiety, travelled to Bunbury to see if there was any news of the whaler. There was none. Bitterly disappointed, he returned to Fremantle.

Awaiting him was another serious problem. Two strangers had arrived in the town and were watching the prison. John King suspected that they were British spies. King had also learned that yet another plot to free the prisoners was being planned. If the British had learned of this plot, it would explain why the two strangers were watching the prison.

Breslin realised that it was imperative to find out who the strangers were and what they were up to. King suggested that he should make contact with the men, find out who they were and what they were doing in Fremantle.

This was a dangerous undertaking. If they were British spies King would be arrested and thrown into Fremantle Prison. However, if they were IRB men plotting to rescue the prisoners, they might suspect that King was a British spy and kill him.

Despite these dangers, and aware that whether the men were spies or IRB men they would be armed, King stopped one of them one night. 'Who are you?' he demanded. 'What are you doing in Fremantle?'

The man was clearly alarmed. 'I'm . . . I'm Dennis McCarthy,' he stuttered. 'I'm . . . I'm helping my uncle on his farm.'

'No, you're not,' King said. 'You're an IRB man and you're plotting to free the six Fenian prisoners. I'm also an IRB man and I'm willing to help you. But first you must prove to me that you are an IRB man.'

McCarthy now admitted to being an IRB man. He also admitted that his companion, a man named Walsh, was in the IRB, too. 'I can prove this,' he said to King. 'Meet me on the beach and I will show you the proof.'

King agreed. 'Within the hour,' he said, as he walked away.

King knew that he was taking a great risk in meeting McCarthy on a quiet beach. If McCarthy brought Walsh with him King would be outnumbered. The two men could murder him and throw his body into the ocean to be eaten by sharks.

King waited on the beach. Within the hour he saw a lone man approaching. As he drew near, King recognised McCarthy. The latter now showed King written orders he had received from the IRB authorising him to free the Fenian prisoners. He also gave King a secret IRB password. 'We have a large sum of money,' he explained. 'We're going to bribe a whaling captain to take the prisoners on board.'

King hesitated. He knew that this plan could jeopardise the *Catalpa* plan. But could he risk telling McCarthy of that plan? King realised that he had no choice. He now asked McCarthy to come and meet John J. Breslin.

McCarthy agreed and he and Walsh met Breslin later that night. Breslin outlined his rescue plan to the two men and suggested that they give up their own plan and help with the *Catalpa* plan.

Are British Spies Watching?

Both men agreed and they all shook hands. 'All we care about is that the prisoners should be freed,' McCarthy said.

'You must cut the telegraph lines on the day of the rescue,' Breslin now said. 'News of the escape must not be sent from Fremantle. It will buy us vital time before the authorities can send police and soldiers or put the navy on our trail.'

Both men nodded. 'It will be done,' Walsh said. 'Now when is the *Catalpa* due in Bunbury?'

'Soon,' Breslin said confidently. 'She will be here soon.'

As the two men left, King stared at Breslin. Both their faces were dark with anxiety. Neither man spoke his thoughts aloud though each guessed what the other was thinking. When would the *Catalpa* reach Bunbury? Would she do so before a British spy learned of the plan and the prisoners were moved to work gangs far from Fremantle? Or else locked up securely within the walls of Fremantle Prison, from which they would have no hope of escape?

Breslin knew that time was running out and, with it, all hope.

17

The *Catalpa* Docks

During all this time, Captain Anthony had problems of his own. Shortly after meeting Cozens, he encountered fierce storms. These were followed by windless days when the *Catalpa* lay motionless on the ocean. The crew grew restless and this increased Anthony's anxiety. He knew he was falling behind schedule, yet there was nothing he could do but hope for good winds.

Eventually, the wind picked up. Anthony ordered that every square centimetre of sail be set. The *Catalpa*, like a thoroughbred horse released from her stall, sped over the waves. The crew, much happier now, began to look forward to reaching New Zealand and going whaling again.

Toward the end of March 1876 a lookout shouted, 'Land ahoy'. The crew crowded the ship's rail to get their first view of what they thought was New Zealand. But the *Catalpa* had reached her true destination – Western Australia. Within 24 hours she would dock in Bunbury. Then the most dangerous phase of the mission could begin.

Each morning during that month of March, Breslin had visited the telegraph office in Fremantle to check if the *Catalpa* had docked in Bunbury. Day after day the news was the same. The *Catalpa* had not arrived. Then on 29 March, Breslin could scarcely believe his eyes as he read the posted notices at the telegraph office. The *Catalpa* had docked in Bunbury the previous day.

A relieved Breslin sent a telegram to John Devoy in America informing him of the ship's arrival. He then sent a telegram to Captain Anthony acknowledging his arrival. Breslin also had a letter smuggled into James Wilson in the prison. It said that a friend had arrived at last, which was code for the arrival of the *Catalpa*. Wilson conveyed the news to his comrades. At last, freedom was within their grasp.

Breslin now took the coach to Bunbury to meet with Captain Anthony. By a stroke of luck, a local businessman introduced the two men. This made their meeting seem natural and unsuspicious. They discussed the plan to free the prisoners and Anthony agreed to travel with Breslin to Fremantle to take a look at Rockingham beach. But before they could leave they encountered a new problem.

Thomas Brennan now arrived in Bunbury and demanded to be included in the escape plan. Though Breslin and Anthony knew that Brennan might cause problems, they had no choice but to agree to his demand.

The three men now took the steamer, *Georgette*, to Fremantle. During the voyage, when Captain Grady of the *Georgette* learned that a whaling captain was on board, he insisted on meeting him. Now Anthony had an opportunity to find out as much information about the coastline as possible.

Grady showed Anthony his charts of the coastline, including those for the Rockingham beach area. Grady knew the coastline well and was able to point out certain hazards that could pose problems for a ship, especially the shoals around Garden Island.

Anthony took careful note of all this information, aware that it might yet prove useful.

Breslin and Anthony, as befitting two new-found American friends, met often during the voyage to chat. Anthony informed Breslin that he could foresee no problem with Rockingham beach as the rendezvous point. Everything seemed to be going well. Even Brennan, who was warned to treat the two men as strangers during the journey, did what he was told.

As the *Georgette* steamed into Fremantle early in April 1876, Breslin was confident that the plan could succeed. As they neared the town, he took Anthony on deck and pointed out to him the massive white fortress that was Fremantle Prison.

At this point, Anthony's heart sank. Could the prisoners ever escape from such a fortress, he wondered? He voiced his doubts aloud, but Breslin assured him that it was possible. 'We will succeed,' Breslin said. 'I can't foresee any problem that might arise to deny us success.'

But as the steamer pulled into Fremantle dock, both men received a terrible shock. Tied up at the quay was a British warship. She was a fast gunboat, the HMS *Conflict*, and she was heavily armed.

It was the worst possible sight that could have greeted the two men. If word of the escape plan reached the authorities, the *Conflict* could intervene and prevent the rescue. Even if the *Catalpa* sailed away with the six prisoners, the *Conflict* could easily overtake her. If that happened, the unarmed *Catalpa* would be no match for the British cannons. She would have no choice but to surrender.

Now the presence of the warship posed the greatest threat to the whole plan. Both men suspected that her presence was not a coincidence. The authorities must have learned of the plot, or at least had their suspicions aroused.

And now the question had to be considered if there was an informer among them? When they put their plan into action, would soldiers be lying in wait? Rather than freeing the six Fenians, would they all end up as prisoners themselves?

Tied up at the quay was a British warship, HMS Conflict.

DES SCANLON, AGED 16

18

The Rescue in Peril

All the conspirators now met at the Emerald Isle Hotel to discuss the situation. They agreed that they could not go ahead with the plan while *Conflict* was in Fremantle. If she remained in port, then the plan would have to be abandoned.

From locals, they learned that the ship was on an annual visit to Fremantle and would leave again within a week. Yet they could not be certain if this was so. All they could do now was wait and see.

Waiting for even a week was posing a particularly difficult problem for Anthony. His crew suspected that something was wrong, and were on the verge of mutiny. Some of them had gone ashore without permission, but had been recaptured. Three of them were now were clapped in irons on the *Catalpa*. A fourth crewman was in Bunbury lock-up.

Anthony knew that if he remained in Bunbury and did not go whaling, the authorities would become suspicious. Questions would be asked as to why the *Catalpa* was in the area. During this time, Duggan was constructing new cabins on the *Catalpa's* deck. This, too, was likely to arouse suspicion with the authorities. Brennan posed yet another problem. An impetuous man, he might do something foolish while they waited.

The Rescue in Peril

During this enforced wait, Anthony surveyed the area at Rockingham beach. He thought it would suit their purpose perfectly. He marked the spot with stakes driven into the sand. These would help to locate the exact spot when a whaleboat from the *Catalpa* picked up the prisoners from the beach.

Now, to Anthony's dismay, he and Breslin were invited to dine with Governor Robinson. Anthony had no choice but to travel to Perth. If he did not, it might arouse suspicion.

The dinner was an unpleasant experience for Anthony, who was questioned closely about his reasons for being in Bunbury. He explained that he was on his way to New Zealand to hunt whales, hoping that he was believed. When the dinner was over, he was relieved to get back to Fremantle and decided to return to Bunbury right away. He would wait there for news from Breslin that the *Conflict* had sailed.

On 11 April 1876, the *Conflict* raised anchor and, under full sail, left Fremantle. A relieved Breslin immediately telegraphed Anthony with the news. Once he received it, he contacted the authorities to obtain permission to sail.

Anthony intended to sail on Thursday 13 April with the escape attempt to take place on Friday 14 April. But that Friday was Good Friday. It was a holiday in Western Australia, and because of this, the prisoners would be confined to their cells all day. The escape would have to be postponed until Saturday.

Fate seemed to be conspiring against them. A fierce storm now blew up. Howling winds and driving rain lashed the *Catalpa*. The storm was so severe that she dragged her anchors and was in danger of being driven onto a sandbank. Though Captain Anthony's expert seamanship saved her, she could not now sail as arranged.

Frantic telegrams went back and forth between Anthony and Breslin. Tom Desmond was told to wait in Perth for further word. McCarthy and Walsh had to be prevented from cutting the telegraph lines. If they were cut, the authorities would be forewarned that something was afoot.

Word was also got to the prisoners that the escape attempt had to be called off. This was terrible news. The men had placed all their hopes on the plan. Now that hope was being dashed.

They also had an added worry to contend with. A rumour claimed that the six Fenians were about to be sent to work gangs in the bush. It seemed the authorities were at last taking the information of an IRB rescue plot to heart.

With the plan unable to proceed on the Saturday or Sunday, it was now set for Easter Monday, 17 April. When Anthony telegraphed Breslin to confirm that the *Catalpa* would be waiting off Rockingham beach on Monday, Breslin frantically contacted all the conspirators.

Desmond was told to return to Fremantle with horses and a carriage. Brennan was to hire or borrow horses and a trap. McCarthy and Walsh were instructed to be ready to cut the telegraph lines. John King was told to obtain a fast horse for the day while Breslin himself arranged to hire horses and a carriage.

Word was got to the prisoners through James Wilson. 'Monday is the day,' he told them. 'We will either escape on that day or we will die. Whatever happens, we will never spend another night in this godforsaken prison.'

Yet despite Wilson's words, it was with great anxiety that the prisoners heard the iron doors of their cells clang shut on Easter Sunday night. Once more, they were locked in their tombs. Now, they could only hope and pray that it was for the last time.

19

Breakers Ahead!

On Easter Sunday, the *Catalpa* hove to in international waters off Rockingham beach. Anthony ordered a whaleboat to be provisioned and chose five men to accompany him. His plan was to row to the rendezvous point and wait there overnight for the prisoners.

Anthony now said goodbye to Sam Smith, his loyal First Mate. 'If anything should go wrong, or if I'm arrested, you get away in the *Catalpa*,' he told Smith, as the two men shook hands. 'You can then decide what to do.'

Smith nodded and wished Anthony well. The captain took a last long around his ship, which had served him well. The crew, too, for the most part had been loyal even though they were unsettled by the long delay in returning to whaling.

Anthony climbed into the whaleboat along with the five men. Once they were settled at the oars with Anthony at the tiller, he gave the order, 'Lower away.' To the creaking of pulley wheels, the boat was lowered down the side of the *Catalpa* into the Indian Ocean.

As the boat dropped toward the water, Anthony had very mixed emotions. He knew that this was the most dangerous part of the plan. If the British authorities had learned of the plan, or

'Man the oars,' ordered Captain Anthony.

WAYNE MCCARTHY, AGED 14

if there was an informer among the plotters, he and his crew would be arrested. They would find themselves in Fremantle Prison where he knew that he would be treated harshly. What was even worse to contemplate was that he might never see his wife or daughter again.

Once on the water, Anthony called out the order, 'Man the oars'. The men pulled together and the whaleboat crested a wave and drew away from the ship. From the deck of the *Catalpa*, Smith watched her until she was little more than a dark speck on the blue ocean.

With a favourable breeze blowing, Anthony ordered that the sail be hoisted. Now the boat skimmed the waves and the men relaxed. Anthony, however, did not relax. As the boat neared shore, he scanned the area with his telescope for signs of danger. There appeared to be none.

But danger lurked all around them. Sharks continually circled the boat, their dark fins slicing through the water. Anyone unlucky enough to end up in the ocean would stand little chance against the ferocious predators.

Suddenly, danger came from another source. The men heard a sound like thunder and a warning shout went up, 'Breakers ahead!'

'Man the oars!' Anthony barked, but the experienced crewmen had already done so.

The warning shout had come just in time. Huge waves now struck the boat and lifted her into the air. Another wave struck and whirled her round. Water poured over the gunwales, threatening to swamp her. The men on board could only hang on and hope. If she capsized or sank, all was lost.

The boat now crashed down into the water, jarring everyone

on board. But she remained upright. She had also cleared the rocks, which had caused the breakers. The men were soaked, but otherwise unharmed. Slowly they recovered from their fright and from swallowing seawater.

Anthony now checked the beach once more through his telescope. There was no obvious sign of danger. He also located the stakes with which he had marked the spot where he intended to land. But he decided to wait until dark before doing so.

As darkness fell, he ordered the men to pull for shore. Eventually the boat's keel scraped against sand. They had made it. Anthony had the boat pulled up on to the beach and camouflaged with grass and twigs. Then they all ate. Afterwards, the men settled themselves in the long shore grass and were soon snoring. Anthony could not sleep and prowled the beach all night.

It was also a long night for all those others involved in the plan. On the *Catalpa*, Sam Smith lay awake listening to the creak of the ship's timbers as she rode the waves. Breslin and the other Irishmen slept fitfully, aware that it might be their last night of freedom.

For the six Fenian prisoners, it was worst of all. As they looked up at the small patches of moonlight shining through the windows in their cells, they knew that at long last freedom lay within their reach.

20

More Danger Looms

Dawn eventually broke over Rockingham beach. As the sun peeped above the horizon Captain Anthony woke his men. To the sound of birdsong, they lit a fire and cooked a meagre breakfast.

As yet, the men did not know the real purpose of their mission, or that it might entail great danger. Anthony worried as to what their reaction would be when the prisoners arrived at the beach. But this worry quickly faded when Anthony realised that danger threatened from another source.

It was with alarm that he noted a jetty a little way along from where he and his crew were waiting. A sign denoted it as belonging to the Jarrah Timber Company. Already men were at work there, unloading timber from a wagon.

Anthony anxiously scanned the horizon, but there was no sign of an approaching ship. Could the timber be for a British warship, he wondered? If one were to arrive, then the rescue would have to be abandoned.

One of the workmen spotted Anthony and approached him. He was clearly suspicious of the presence of Anthony and his men. The man introduced himself as William Bell. 'Who are you?' he demanded. 'What are you doing here?'

'I'm a whaling skipper,' Anthony said. 'I lost an anchor in the storm. We're on our way to Fremantle to buy a new one.'

Bell shook his head. 'You're deserters from a whaler,' he said. 'I can tell.'

Anthony waited. If Bell called out a warning to his work colleagues then all was lost. They would raise the alarm and within hours the beach would be swarming with police. If Anthony and his crew were still here then, they would be arrested.

Anthony had brought his revolver with him and knew that he could shoot Bell. But he could never be party to violence. And he could not shoot the other men who were now watching from the jetty.

Just when Anthony thought that all was lost, Bell smiled. 'You've nothing to fear from me,' he said. 'I've done time in prison. I just came to warn you to clear out right away. The *Georgette* is due here this morning to pick up timber.'

Bell turned and, shading his eyes, stared out to sea. 'There she comes now,' he said, pointing.

Anthony stared toward where Bell indicated. On the horizon, he saw a dark smudged line, drawn as if with a pencil on the blue sky. It was smoke from the steamer. She would arrive in a few hours at most. Anthony's heart sank. He would have to get the prisoners off the beach in the next hour or all was lost.

'Well, good luck,' Bell said, and with that he returned to the jetty.

Anthony had now to deal with his suspicious crewmen. Bell's presence had alarmed them. They were worried that they would be arrested as deserters. Anthony assured them that this would not happen.

More Danger Looms

'We're here to pick up some men who wish to travel to America,' he said. 'You have nothing to fear.' As he spoke, he wondered again how they would react when the prisoners arrived. When that happened, his men would know that police would be searching for the escapees. Anyone caught helping them would be arrested and imprisoned.

Anthony also worried about the workmen on the jetty. Once they learned of the escape, they would inform the police of the presence of himself and his men. He also knew that the authorities would quickly figure out that they were from the *Catalpa*. Then they would begin a hunt for the whaler. The *Georgette* was certain to be on their tail within hours.

For now, there was nothing Anthony could do but wait. With one eye on the smoke from the *Georgette*, he listened for the pounding of hooves, which would signal the arrival of the prisoners.

He was aware that it might be the sound of gunfire he would hear. If the escape went wrong, armed police and warders would be sent in pursuit of the fleeing prisoners. If that happened, Anthony and his crew could be caught up in a gun battle and killed. The rescue, which he had hoped would be straight-forward, could now become both dangerous and deadly.

As for the six Fenian prisoners, they were all determined that this would be their last night in prison. Never again would they be entombed. When their cell doors opened tomorrow morning, they would gain their freedom, or die in the attempt.

21

Prisoners Escape

While Anthony waited at Rockingham beach, the other men involved in the rescue were going about their allotted tasks. Brennan left Fremantle early that morning in a two-wheeled trap with luggage and weapons. Tom Desmond, in a four-wheeled trap, headed for a pre-arranged rendezvous point on the Rockingham road.

Both the IRB men, McCarthy and Walsh, also left Fremantle early that morning. They were carrying wire cutters to cut the telegraph wires, which would prevent news of the escape being sent from Fremantle.

Breslin left his hotel early and made his way to nearby stables. Here, he found a four-wheeled trap and horses waiting for him. He, too, now set off to meet up with Desmond. They would wait at the rendezvous point until 9 a.m. If the prisoners had not arrived by then, they would have to abandon the plan.

John King remained in Fremantle. He had acquired a fast horse and would wait behind for some time to see if the alarm was raised. Then he would race to Rockingham beach with the news.

Breslin joined Desmond at the rendezvous point and shared out clothing for the prisoners, along with guns. Then they pulled off the road to hide from prying eyes. From their hiding place they watched the prison from which six desperate men would attempt to escape.

The prisoners had been awake long before dawn. After parade and breakfast they set about their escape plan. Michael Harrington walked with other prisoners to the docks, where they were carrying out repairs. Thomas Darragh made his way to the clerk of work's garden to dig potatoes. Thomas Hassett and Robert Cranston told the guard on the main gate that they, too, had been assigned to dig potatoes. The unsuspicious guard gave them permission to leave the prison.

Both James Wilson and Martin Hogan were already outside the walls. Wilson worked in the prison chaplain's stables. Hogan was painting a house in the town. Now all six men were outside the prison and ready to go on to the next part of the plan.

While Hassett went off to the potato garden to meet up with Darragh, Cranston walked to the docks. Here he told the warder in charge that Harrington was needed to move furniture at the Governor's house. The warder gave Harrington permission to go with Cranston. Both men set off together, not to the Governor's house, but toward the potato garden.

On the way they met Wilson, who had slipped away from the stables. The three men now made their way toward the Rockingham road. Meanwhile, Darragh and Hassett had set off to meet up with Hogan. He joined them and the three men also headed for the Rockingham road to meet Breslin and Desmond.

On seeing the waiting traps, the six prisoners broke into a run. When they reached the traps, they leaped on board, three to each trap. There was little time for greetings or celebration. Within moments both traps were hurtling down the road, leaving a dust trail in their wake.

The *Catalpa* Adventure

While the traps sped on, the prisoners quickly changed out of their loathed Drogheda linens and put on civilian clothing. Now they grabbed revolvers and checked the weapons, determined to fight to remain free, or to die in the attempt.

22

Police in Pursuit

On Rockingham beach, an anxious Captain Anthony watched the smoke from the *Georgette*. To his relief, she was still far out at sea. But he had another problem to consider. The wind was increasing in strength, indicating that a storm was brewing. It would make the return trip to the *Catalpa*, in an overloaded whaleboat, doubly dangerous.

Suddenly, a seaman shouted: 'Horses coming.' Moments later Tom Brennan drew up on the beach. As he did so, William Bell rushed over from the jetty to see what was happening and Brennan wanted to shoot him. 'I'm in charge here,' Anthony said. 'There will be no shooting unless I give the order.'

Brennan backed down and began to unload the luggage. Bell's astonishment turned to fear and suspicion when he spotted the rifles and revolvers in the trap. Before he could react, the pounding hooves of a galloping horse were heard. Moments later, John King rode on to the beach and pulled his sweating, dusty horse to a halt. 'The alarm has not yet been raised,' King shouted to Anthony. 'Breslin and Desmond will be here soon.'

'We have a problem,' Anthony shouted, pointing toward where smoke lay black against a darkening sky. 'The *Georgette*'s coming here to pick up timber.'

King realised the seriousness of the situation. 'I'll ride back,' he said, 'and urge Breslin and Desmond to hurry.' He pulled his horse around and galloped away.

By now, Anthony's crewmen were becoming alarmed. Again he reassured them, and ordered them to drag the boat to the water's edge. 'Stand by,' he said, 'and launch the boat when I give the order.' The men obeyed, but continued to watch Bell and Brennan with growing apprehension.

Minutes passed, but still there was no sign of the prisoners. By now the sky had darkened considerably and the squally wind was growing stronger and colder. Anthony's anxiety was increasing by the minute.

Again they heard the drumming of horses' hooves. Moments later, King, followed by the two traps, raced on to the beach. They hurtled up to the waiting group, the horses lathered in sweat and covered in dust and blowing hard. Even as the traps skidded to a stop the prisoners leaped down from them. The six men grabbed rifles and raced toward the waiting whaleboat.

The crewmen were terrified by the sudden appearance of armed men. Some of them were about to run away. Anthony dashed toward them. 'You're not in any danger,' he shouted. 'Stay where you are.'

But the crewmen were still terrified by the wild strangers. They drew knives, prepared to fight. The two groups now confronted each other, the knife-wielding whalers facing the rifles of the prisoners.

Anthony reached the group just in time. 'Lower your guns,' he ordered the prisoners. 'Put your knives away,' he shouted at his crewmen. 'Launch the boat.'

To his relief, both groups obeyed. He knew that if the confrontation had continued, violence would have ensued. The

Again they heard the drumming of horses' hooves.
OKTAWIA BOGUSZ, AGED 15

prisoners, having their first taste of freedom in years, were not in any mood to give it up. They would have fought to the death rather than return to their 'tombs' in Fremantle Prison.

When the boat was launched, the prisoners and their rescuers scrambled in. Anthony leaped in last and ordered his crew to pull with all their might. They found it difficult to get the overloaded boat moving. But Anthony shouted encouragement and slowly the boat pulled away from the shore.

As it did so, William Bell mounted John King's horse and galloped back toward Fremantle. Those on the whaleboat knew that if the alarm hadn't already been raised then it soon would be. Armed police would quickly be here. Anthony glanced at the smoke from the steamer. She was still some distance away, but drawing nearer.

The wind was still stiffening and dark clouds were ominously gathering. The storm was about to break. Unaware of this, the six prisoners and those who had helped them escape were celebrating their success.

But their jubilation changed to alarm when they saw mounted police riding hard along the Rockingham road. They charged on to the beach and leapt down from their panting horses. At the water's edge, they raised their rifles to their shoulders.

A volley of shots rang out and those on the boat ducked low. But the bullets went wide. After a few fruitless volleys, the firing ceased. Anthony urged his men to pull harder.

They didn't need much urging and soon the whaleboat was out of range of the policemen's rifles. They remounted their horses, and to the cheers of the prisoners, galloped back toward Fremantle.

Police in Pursuit

Now John J. Breslin took a sheet of paper from his pocket. It was a letter to the authorities. It stated that on this day he had released from Her Majesty's Prison six Fenian prisoners harshly convicted and imprisoned for love of their country.

While the prisoners wept and the tough whaling men stared at them, Breslin put the letter in a waterproof wrapper. He then tied this to a piece of wood and cast it on the water. The wind and tide would carry it to the shore.

The prisoners cheered again, relishing their new-found freedom. As Anthony looked at them, he saw jubilation on their faces. They thought the worst was over but he knew this was not so. The *Georgette* was drawing closer to shore. Once she arrived, Anthony knew that the authorities would send her in hot pursuit of the whaleboat and the *Catalpa*.

Anthony knew he was in a race against time. It was a race against not only the *Georgette*, but against the worsening weather. It was a race he had to win. If he lost, then he and those on the whaleboat would either drown or be brought to Fremantle in chains.

23
Another Storm Rages

At around 10 a.m. that morning, the alarm was raised at the prison. Soon the news spread throughout the town that six Fenian prisoners had escaped. The authorities tried to send a telegram to order HMS *Conflict* to pursue the escapees. But the telegraph lines had been cut.

Panic and confusion ensued. At first, no one knew what to do. Inquiries then established that horses and traps had been seen racing toward Rockingham. Mounted police were sent in pursuit, but reached Rockingham beach too late to recapture the prisoners or those who had helped them escape.

Riders were now sent to Perth with the news. When Governor Robinson was told, he came straight to Fremantle. Here, he learned of the *Catalpa*'s presence in Bunbury, and of the role that the American, 'Mr Collins', had played in the escape.

Little could be done until the telegraph lines were repaired. Once this was done, telegrams were sent to Perth, Albany, and other places. By now, William Bell had also told the police what he knew.

Superintendent Stone, head of the water police, sent a police boat to look for any sign of the whaleboat, or the *Catalpa*. He also ordered a contingent of armed police and pensioner guards to be ready to board the *Georgette* as soon as she docked.

Another Storm Rages

Later that day, Detective Rowe arrived from Perth. Rowe was hopeful that HMS *Conflict* might yet be able to pursue *Catalpa*. But he was disappointed to learn that the warship had already sailed from Albany, and could not be contacted.

Now Rowe and Superintendent Stone realised that they would have to rely on the *Georgette* to try and recapture the prisoners. Unable to contact Captain Grady to tell him to hurry, they could only wait for the steamer to dock.

Meanwhile, Governor Robinson had sent a telegram to all naval stations and ports in Australia. It stated that the *Catalpa* was to be detained if found and everyone on board arrested.

Now the Governor could only wait. He knew that if all his efforts failed, then the *Catalpa*, her crew, the prisoners and those who had aided them, would escape. There was nothing else he could do to prevent it.

What the Governor had not taken into consideration was the weather. Now, as efforts to find those involved in the escape were set in motion, the whaleboat was battling winds and rough seas. As it passed the reefs, which had nearly sunk it the previous night, Anthony and his crew suppressed a shiver. Seeing the jagged rocks, they realised how close they had come to disaster.

Anthony now ordered the sail to be raised. But as the wind increased, it had to be taken down. The boat was dangerously low in the water and was in danger of being swamped. As dark clouds roiled across the sky, Anthony knew that the storm was about to hit them. And, as yet, there was no sign of the *Catalpa*.

Anthony tried to hide his apprehension. But soon the prisoners and the other Irishmen began to sense the tension in the sailors. The waves were becoming higher as the wind increased. Seawater was cascading into the boat. No one needed Anthony to confirm that trouble was brewing.

Then to everyone's relief, they saw the dark hull of a ship in the distance. 'It's the *Catalpa*,' Anthony shouted above the roar of the wind and the crash of the waves. 'Pull harder, men! We're almost home.'

The tired oarsmen hardly needed urging. They bent their backs to the oars and pulled with all their might. Anthony ordered the sail to be raised again and, much to everyone's relief, they began to gain on the ship. But now water was pouring into the boat with every wave that struck her.

'Start bailing,' Anthony ordered the Irishmen, who needed no further urging. But now the light was fading and this, coupled with sheeting rain, was hampering visibility. They lost sight of *Catalpa*, glimpsing her only now and then as their boat and the ship rose and fell on the lengthening swell.

Anthony still kept the sail raised, though he knew it was becoming more dangerous. But he felt he had no choice. He did not wish to spend a night on the ocean in the open boat. If forced to do so, there was a good chance that they would all die.

Just when they were certain that they would reach the *Catalpa*, disaster struck. A vicious gust struck the whaleboat and snapped the mast, dangerously rocking the boat. Water cascaded over the gunwales. By now some of the Irishmen were seasick, unused to such violent movement.

The crew were all seasoned sailors. They knew that they had to act quickly. Even as Anthony bellowed, 'Cut the ropes!' the men grabbed hatchets or whaling knives. They hacked at the ropes fastening the sail to the mast before the boat capsized. As they did so, further torrents of water swept over the gunwales.

The tired oarsmen pulled with all their might on the oars.

SHARLENE CASEY, AGED 14

Just in time, the crew managed to cut the sail free and drag it into the boat. Then they grabbed the oars again and began to row with all their strength, desperate to keep the boat head-on into the waves. Those Irishmen who weren't seasick bailed furiously, aware that all their lives were at risk.

But then a terrible cry of despair rent the air. For a moment, among the sheets of rain, which was adding to everyone's discomfort, a crewman had glimpsed the *Catalpa*'s mast lights. 'Captain,' he cried out, '*Catalpa*'s heading out to sea.'

Hiding his disappointment and anxiety, Anthony nodded. He knew that Sam Smith, who was now responsible for the safety of the ship and her crew, was taking no risks. Obviously worried about being driven onto the shoals of Garden Island, he was taking the *Catalpa* into open water.

As he glimpsed *Catalpa* heading away from them, Anthony knew that the last chance of reaching the safety of the ship had gone. They now had to try and survive the storm on the whaleboat. He knew that it was unlikely that they would survive, though he reassured all those on board that they would.

But fear gripped even the seasoned sailors. This fear transferred itself to all on board. As monstrous waves continued to toss the boat about, and as the wind chilled the soaking-wet occupants, they all believed that they would drown this night. Sharks would devour their flesh, leaving their bones to litter the bed of the Indian Ocean, tens of thousands of kilometres from their homes and their families.

24

The Longest Night of All

When the *Georgette* docked, Governor Robinson ordered Superintendent Stone to pursue the prisoners. Stone picked eighteen pensioner guards and eight policemen to accompany him on the steamer.

Despite the storm, the *Georgette* cast off her mooring lines late that Monday evening and headed out to sea. Throughout the night she ploughed through the waves toward where Captain Grady thought the *Catalpa* might be. The ship pitched and rolled in gigantic seas, while the wind howled like a demon in the rigging. Those on board were fearful at times, but at least they were protected from the worst of the elements.

But those in the open whaleboat had no such protection. As the storm raged through the night, they were battered by wind and rain. Captain Anthony ordered their food and water to be thrown overboard to lighten the boat. The empty water casks were then used for bailing.

Throughout the night the men rowed and bailed, desperately trying to keep the tiny craft afloat. As the hours passed and the men wearied, Anthony encouraged them. 'We'll make it,' he told them. 'I've survived worse storms than this.'

In truth, he and his crew had survived worse storms. But they had not done so in an overloaded whaleboat. Even with just the five crewmen and Anthony on board, it would have been difficult to keep the craft afloat. But with ten extra men, it was proving almost impossible.

The previous night had been a long one for Captain Anthony. But this night now was proving to be the longest of his life. He knew that if he and those with him survived, they could count themselves the luckiest men on earth.

As the night wore on, their luck held out. Then just before dawn Anthony sensed that the wind was dropping. Soon, his experience told him that the storm was abating. As dawn broke, the storm blew itself out. Renewed hope rose in the men's hearts. It gave them fresh courage. Though they were hungry and thirsty and wet and cold and terribly tired, they were grateful to be alive.

Then, as if to lift their spirits further, they glimpsed sails on the horizon. It was the *Catalpa*! She was heading toward them. It was just the boost they needed, and though no man felt like cheering aloud, inwardly they all cheered.

Then John J. Breslin gave a shout of alarm that struck all of them with fear. They stared at Breslin, who was pointing back toward the shore. 'There's a ship,' he said. 'It's heading this way.'

Eyes weary from lack of sleep and exhaustion, and stung by salt water, peered in the direction of his pointing finger. Some of the men rubbed their eyes, thinking that what they were seeing was perhaps just a streak of dark cloud.

But as they strained their eyes, they knew that it was no cloud. What was streaking the brightening dawn sky was a smudge of dark smoke. A ship, almost certainly the *Georgette*, was in hot pursuit of them.

For a moment every man on the boat, including Captain Anthony, was stunned into silence. Then Anthony reacted in the manner of the great captain that he was. 'Pull, men!' he ordered. 'Row for your lives! If we don't reach the safety of the *Catalpa*, we'll all be clapped in chains.'

The sailors did not need prompting. Facing the prospect of prison, and though exhausted, they found new strength. Hauling with all their might on their oars, they pulled in unison. Their eyes, like those of every man on the whaleboat, alternately looked toward the *Catalpa* and then back toward the pursuer.

The rowers grunted from their exertions. All the time Anthony called out words of encouragement. The oars cut through the water, powering the whaleboat toward what they all hoped was sanctuary.

But they could all see that the pursuing ship, which they now recognised as the *Georgette*, was gaining on them. She was closing in on the whaleboat more quickly than they were closing the gap between themselves and the *Catalpa*. Anthony ordered the makeshift sail to be raised. But still they could not gain on the *Catalpa*, which was now moving away from them.

What they did not know was that Sam Smith had not seen their whaleboat. But he had seen the *Georgette* approaching, and had decided to take the *Catalpa* further out to sea. By doing so, he had left the whaleboat at the mercy of the fast approaching *Georgette*. At the very last moment, was the rescue about to fail?

25

Race to Freedom

While the sailors rowed for their lives, the Irishmen on the whaleboat prepared to fight. They grabbed their rifles and reloaded them with dry cartridges. They were determined to die rather than be captured.

This possibility seemed ever more likely. As the *Catalpa* drew further away, the *Georgette* continued to close the gap to the whaleboat. Now, the hunted men could see the lookouts on her deck.

'Take down the sail,' Anthony ordered. 'Everyone crouch down. Maybe the lookouts won't see us.'

Luck was once more on their side. The *Georgette* passed them, clearly intent on catching up with the *Catalpa*. 'Follow the *Georgette*,' Anthony now ordered. 'No one will be looking out for us at the stern.'

The crew began to pull again in the wake of the *Georgette*. But she was much too fast for them. They were left behind, as she headed at full speed toward the *Catalpa*.

When the *Georgette* reached the *Catalpa*, Superintendent Stone ordered Grady to pull alongside the whaler. Stone now hollered across to Sam Smith, who was on deck, and demanded to know if the escaped prisoners were on board.

'No, they are not,' Sam Smith answered truthfully.

'Where is your missing whaleboat?' Stone demanded.

'Captain's taken her to Fremantle to buy a new anchor,' Smith lied. 'We lost it in the storm.'

'I'm going to come on board,' Stone yelled. 'I'm going to search your ship for six escaped prisoners.'

At this point Smith grabbed a harpoon. 'This is an American ship,' he stated firmly. 'I will not allow you on board.'

Stone hesitated. By law, he was not allowed to board the vessel without permission. As he mulled over what he should do, he found that there was another problem. Grady informed him that the steamer was running low on coal, and would have to return to Fremantle to take on new supplies.

Stone had to accept the inevitable and Grady ordered the *Georgette* to head back to Fremantle. This posed further danger for the men on the whaleboat. The steamer was now heading straight toward them. If it did not run them down they would almost certainly be seen.

'Every man down,' Anthony shouted, and they crouched down again. The *Georgette* drew closer. Each man held his breath, as if even that might be seen or heard. The steamer drew still closer. This time the lookouts could hardly avoid seeing the whaleboat, as it passed close by it.

But the *Georgette* steamed past. On the whaleboat, the men breathed sighs of relief. Anthony now ordered the makeshift sail to be raised once more and the men to pull again for their lives.

As the *Georgette* headed back toward Fremantle it encountered a police cutter. On board were heavily armed policemen. Stone ordered them to continue searching for the whaleboat. He now knew it was missing from the *Catalpa* and assumed that those on

The Georgette *gains on the* Catalpa, missing the whaleboat.
CHARLENE LYNCH, AGED 15

board had sought shelter ashore from the storm. They should now be at sea, making their way back to the *Catalpa*.

Though they were exhausted and suffering greatly from hunger and thirst, the sailors pulled hard on their oars. The sight of the nearby *Catalpa* gave them extra strength. But then Tom Desmond shouted a new warning: 'Police boat coming up fast!'

Anthony spotted the boat immediately. He could see that it was crammed with armed policemen. Again, the Irishmen grabbed their rifles, ready to fight. It would be an uneven fight with ten men against at least thirty heavily armed policemen. But the Irishmen were determined to fight to the death.

Captain Anthony had to make a quick decision. Did he take down the sail, have the men lie low again, and hope that the policemen did not see them? Or did he make a run for the *Catalpa*? He had no doubt that if the police boat caught up with them, or cut them off from the *Catalpa* they would all be killed or captured.

Anthony made up his mind. 'Pull, men,' he shouted. 'Pull with all your might.'

From somewhere, the sailors again found reserves of strength. Once more, they rowed with every last ounce of their energy. But it was in vain. The police cutter gained on them in the race to the *Catalpa*. She would cut them off and prevent them from reaching the ship. They would lose the race and their freedom, perhaps even their very lives.

Then those on the whaleboat gave a triumphant yell. The *Catalpa* was swinging about and heading toward them. Both craft were now quickly closing the distance between them.

Captain Anthony shouted encouragement to his crew. But they needed little encouragement. The prospect of salvation, when it seemed that they had been doomed, gave them the impetus they needed.

The whaleboat reached the *Catalpa* on the opposite side to the police boat. Ropes were thrown down from the deck. The men on the whaleboat clambered up the ropes to safety. Meanwhile, sailors hoisted the whaleboat on board. They were just in time. As the boat landed on deck, the police boat raced up to the *Catalpa*.

But it was too late. The policemen, brandishing their rifles, could only look on helplessly, unable to fire on an American vessel. Some of them recognised Captain Anthony from his time in Fremantle. They also recognised the prisoners and those who had helped them. But there was nothing the police could do. They had lost.

With cheers echoing from the deck of the *Catalpa*, the police boat swung about and headed back to Fremantle. On the *Catalpa*, the jubilation of all those involved in the rescue continued. There were handshakes and slaps on the back as the prisoners celebrated their freedom.

Anthony ordered that a celebratory meal be prepared for all. Extra rations of rum were handed out. Anthony also excused the sailors who had been on the whaleboat from duty for twenty-four hours.

That night the prisoners went on deck along with the men who had helped in their rescue. They had all dreamed of this moment and now, when it was upon them, they could hardly believe it. Standing on the rolling deck, they looked back toward the invisible Australian shore, certain that they would never see it again.

Captain Anthony was also on deck. He watched the prisoners

and sensed their relief and joy. He saw them tilt their faces to catch the light breeze. For men who had spent years virtually entombed, the breeze was a symbol of their new-found freedom.

But it was causing Anthony great anxiety. Above his head, the sails hung slack, the American flag limp. The *Catalpa* was virtually stationary. Lacking favourable wind, for the time being she wasn't going anywhere.

Anthony stared shoreward once more. He knew that the *Georgette* would by now have taken on a full load of coal. Under steam, she would reach the becalmed *Catalpa* by morning. If threatened by her guns, Anthony knew he would have to yield. Perhaps this night was the only night of freedom the prisoners would enjoy. If so, then he, too, was enjoying his last night of freedom. Tomorrow night he might find himself entombed in Fremantle Prison.

26

Surrdender or Die

Anthony's worst fears were realised the next morning. He arrived on deck to see the *Georgette* steaming toward them. Armed soldiers lined the ship's rails. On her deck sat one massive cannon, which was capable of sinking his ship.

Anthony knew he had two choices. He could surrender or he could fight. Now he turned to his crew. 'The men, who have come on board,' he said, 'are escaped prisoners. The *Georgette* is intent on recapturing them. If we surrender, or are taken by force, we will all end up in prison.'

'We will never surrender,' Sam Smith shouted. 'We will fight and die rather than end up in a British prison. Right, men?'

To Anthony's relief his crew yelled their approval. As tough men, used to the freedom of the oceans, they would fight and die rather than face prison. 'Right,' Anthony ordered. 'Get ready to fight. Arm yourselves with every available weapon.'

A harpoon gun was now fixed on the *Catalpa*'s deck. Meanwhile, the sailors armed themselves with harpoons and knives and hatchets. Below decks, the Irishmen cradled rifles, revolvers stuck in their belts. Anthony ordered them to remain out of sight so that he could deny they were on board.

Surrender or Die

The Irishmen watched the *Georgette* approach. For now they obeyed Anthony and remained out of sight. But if it came to a fight, they were ready to rush on deck and do battle or die.

Anthony now watched as a flag was raised on the *Georgette*. It was a signal to stop and lower the sails. He also noted that the breeze was freshening. The sails were filling and the *Catalpa* was gathering speed. Anthony decided to ignore the warning flag.

Then there was a flash from the deck of the *Georgette* and a massive boom. A shot from the cannon passed across the bow of the *Catalpa* and crashed into the sea beyond. Would the next shot smash into the hull of his ship, or land on deck, Anthony wondered? If it did, men would die. But still he gave no order to lower the sails.

Now, the *Georgette* drew alongside the *Catalpa*. 'Heave to,' Superintendent Stone ordered through a speaking trumpet. 'You have escaped prisoners on board.'

'We have no prisoners on board,' Anthony shouted back through his speaking trumpet.

'I can see them on deck,' Stone said. 'I'll give you fifteen minutes to heave to. If you don't obey, I will sink you.' As if to enforce this threat, soldiers were reloading the cannon. Anthony realised that they all faced death.

Anthony had the most difficult decision of his life to make. He knew that the men on board were willing and able to fight. But they could not match that cannon. One shot could break the mast, rendering the *Catalpa* helpless. A shot fired on the deck would kill everyman there.

'This is an American ship,' Anthony shouted. 'She is flying the American flag. It would be an act of war to fire on us.'

'You have escaped prisoners on board,' Stone shouted back.

The Georgette's *cannon aimed at the* Catalpa.
STEPHANIE WILLIAMS, AGED 14

'We intend to board you and arrest them.'

'Do what you like,' Anthony called back and lowered his speaking trumpet. The time for talking was over.

'You have fifteen minutes,' Stone shouted.

Anthony ignored him. Instead, he now noted the *Catalpa*'s

position. She was perilously close to British territorial waters. Once there, the *Georgette* could legally arrest him. Also, he was not taking full advantage of the freshening wind.

'Hard a port,' he shouted to his helmsman, who spun the ship's wheel. This took the *Catalpa* in toward the shore. As the ship changed tack, it seemed as if Anthony was surrendering. Now he barked out new orders. Sailors began to haul in the sails. The *Catalpa* began to slow.

Those on the *Georgette* were jubilant. They were certain that the *Catalpa* was surrendering. Captain Grady now ordered the steamer to heave to so that a boat could be lowered. Stone could then be rowed across to the *Catalpa*, board her and arrest everyone on board.

On the *Catalpa*, Anthony barked out a new order: 'Hard a starboard.' The helmsman spun the ship's wheel again. The *Catalpa* began to swing about, her timbers creaking in protest. 'Hoist the sails!' Anthony shouted. The sailors obeyed and the sails billowed then cracked as the wind filled them. The *Catalpa* swung full about. Now, the wind in her favour, she gathered speed and headed back out to sea.

On the *Georgette*, the sailors and soldiers watched in horror. The *Catalpa* was heading straight toward them, gathering speed all the time. The whaler was going to ram them!

At the last moment, Anthony bellowed: 'Hard a starboard.' The helmsman swung the great wooden wheel. The *Catalpa* heeled over and passed the *Georgette* with just metres to spare. Then, under full sail, she headed out to sea.

Within minutes the *Georgette* had got up steam and came in hot pursuit. But she did not try to overtake the whaler or come alongside her. All those on the *Catalpa* waited with mounting tension for the cannon shot that could cripple her, leaving her to the mercy of the soldiers.

The chase continued in an ever-freshening wind. Every eye on the *Catalpa* stared back at the *Georgette*, watching for the muzzle flash from the cannon. No such flash came.

Then Sam Smith shouted: 'We're gaining on her!'

Anthony trained his telescope on the *Georgette*. She was slowing down. Then she turned about and headed back toward Fremantle. Aware that the *Catalpa* would not surrender without a fight, Superintendent Stone had decided to give up. The chase was over.

It was safe now for the Irishmen to come on deck. Overjoyed that at last their longed-for freedom was firmly in their grasp, they stared at the retreating steamer. Each man now shook Captain Anthony's hand and thanked him, aware that they owed him their freedom and their lives.

He had sailed the *Catalpa* almost 30,000 kilometres across the oceans. He had survived storms and desertions and the scrutiny of suspicious officials. He had sailed into the jaws of the enemy and rescued six living men from their tombs. He had saved them from drowning and, when danger threatened them and his ship, had been willing to fight and die for them. They could not ask more of any man.

As darkness gathered, the *Catalpa* sailed on, carrying to the land of the free the six men she had come to rescue. Thirty thousand kilometres still lay between her and New Bedford. But as if she sensed she was at last going home, she skimmed over the waves with the ease and grace of a seahorse, destined to be remembered as one of the most famous ships of all time.

27
Safe at Last

As the *Catalpa* sailed across the Indian Ocean, Captain Anthony kept a lookout for British warships. He knew that they would have been ordered to search for the *Catalpa* and to detain her if found.

What Anthony didn't know was that the telegraph cable linking Australia to Britain had been cut. News of the escape did not reach London for two weeks. By then, the *Catalpa* was thousands of kilometres from Australia.

But now danger came from another source. Tom Brennan bitterly resented Breslin. He disliked him so much that he began to sow seeds of resentment against him in the prisoners' minds.

Anthony intended going whaling when he reached the South Atlantic. Now Brennan urged the prisoners to oppose this and to take over the ship. He claimed that they needed immediate medical attention and there was the danger that a British warship could still recapture them.

Dennis Duggan, the ship's carpenter, resentful because of his minor role in the rescue, supported Brennan. They now drew up a petition, signed by all the Irishmen except Breslin, demanding that the *Catalpa* sail directly to America or there would be a mutiny.

The *Catalpa* Adventure

Anthony did not want trouble on his ship. He agreed to the demands and set sail for New York. On 19 August 1876, four months after the prisoners escaped from Fremantle Prison, the *Catalpa* sailed into New York Harbour.

When the ship docked, Anthony and Breslin went ashore. While Breslin went to meet the Fenian O'Donovan Rossa to inform him of the arrival of the prisoners, Anthony went to clear customs.

Catalpa sails into New York Harbour.
MURRISSA JOHNSON, AGED 15

Safe at Last

Within the hour, Breslin sent telegrams to John Devoy and other Fenians to tell them the good news. Devoy, who was ill, nevertheless caught a train to New York. All over America, Fenians and their supporters celebrated the good news.

Captain Anthony returned to the *Catalpa*. Already, journalists were swarming around the ship. They were eager to speak to the prisoners and all those involved in the daring rescue. While the *Catalpa* had been making her way to America, the story of the escape had been front-page news.

Once on board, Anthony spoke to the six prisoners. 'You are now free men,' he told them. 'You can go ashore whenever you wish.'

Later that day the six prisoners disembarked from the *Catalpa*. Before they climbed down into the boat, which would take them to Manhattan, each man shook Anthony's hand and thanked him. They all knew that they owed him their freedom.

Later, as they stepped ashore in America, each man gave thanks for his deliverance. The dream they had harboured for so long was at long last a reality. Never again would they hear the slam of a prison door. Never again would they be put in chains. Now they were as free as the colourful parrots and cockatoos they had once seen flitting about in the Australian bush.

While the prisoners and their supporters celebrated their success, the *Catalpa* sailed from New York on 22 August. Two days later, on 24 August, with Anthony on deck and the loyal Sam Smith beside him, the *Catalpa*, battered by her sixteen months at sea, sailed into New Bedford Harbour.

Hundreds of cheering people lined the quayside. Huge guns boomed out a salute from above the harbour. As Anthony drew near the quayside he saw his wife, Emma, and daughter, Sophie, waiting for him. With them were John T. Richardson and Henry C. Hathaway. The sight was too much for Anthony. Overcome with emotion, he wept like a child.

Those awaiting Anthony hardly recognised him. He had lost weight and his thick dark hair had thinned, and was now tinged with grey. After a tumultuous welcome, Anthony, Emma and Sophie got into a carriage and headed home.

As they pulled away from the quayside, Anthony took one last look back. Battered as he himself was, the *Catalpa* lay quietly at anchor. They had been through much together and the ship had proven herself worthy. One day soon she would slip her moorings again and head out into the Atlantic. But Anthony knew his seafaring days were over. He had made his final voyage.

He now took his wife's delicate hand in one of his coarse seaman's hands. In his other hand, he grasped the tiny hand of his daughter. With his family beside him, he was going home at last.

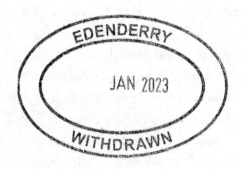